POISON PASSION

POISON PASSION

LINDA JORDAN

METAMORPHOSIS PRESS

Published by Metamorphosis Press

www.MetamorphosisPress.com

ISBN-13: 978-0997797169

For Michael & Zoe

Georgina Wetherby stood in her bedroom, looking back and forth between the open closet and the rolling suitcase on her bed. It was filled with orange, white and black fur. Her two Maine Coon cats, sleeping. They knew she was going away and were sticking close.

She sat down on the soft bed, which sagged way too much. It didn't really matter that they'd taken up the entire suitcase. She had no idea what to pack. Alice, the orange and white furry ball began purring loudly.

Gina fingered the lilacs in a glass vase sitting on her bleached wood nightstand. She'd picked them two days ago, but their scent still perfumed the entire room. She closed her eyes, taking the smell in. There was nothing quite like lilacs to take her back to her childhood.

She opened her eyes. Right. Focus on the problem at hand.

The trip was only four days. Paul, her client, had said dress should be casual. So three pairs of jeans, two pairs of capris. T-shirts and a sweater to round things out. Sandals, sneakers, a pair of rubbery shoes. And her rain coat and hat, because this was the Pacific Northwest and even though the weather people forecast the next week as sunny, it could and probably would, rain. It was only May, after all.

Gina rose and began pulling clothes from hangers and shelves. Maybe one dressier outfit. Just in case they had a different idea of what casual meant. Okay, maybe two. And a couple of long sleeved t-shirts.

She piled the clothes on the bed and began rolling them up. Still nowhere to put them. Maybe she should get a decoy suitcase. No, the cats would only split up. Devious creatures. She'd go do something else until they left.

Gina went into the room that was her studio.

The large framed painting was already packed in plastic bubble wrapping and a wooden box that her neighbor Gene had made. He said it would withstand rough handling. She'd thanked him, promising him and Bev a painting in return.

She hauled the painting into the living room and returned to the studio. Quickly gathering together her paints, brushes, a new 8" x 10" watercolor block, her folding easel and other painting supplies. Stuffing them into the large khaki-colored canvas bag she used when painting outside of the house. Then took that to the living room and closed the door to her studio. No cats allowed without a chaperone. She needed to grab a water bottle from the kitchen to fill up the paint brush jar.

She probably should clean up the house too, but it was just Shelley staying here. She'd seen her mom's messes before.

Gina's cell phone rang and she picked it up off the dining room table. Dining room was sort of a misnomer. Her kitchen, dining room and living room were all one room. The house wasn't large. Just three bedrooms, one bathroom and the great room. It was perfect for her. One story with lovely views from all the windows.

"Hello," she said,

"Are you packed?" asked Melanie.

Melanie Caruthers was her dearest friend. Partly retired, she also lived on Raven Island and they met for dinner or coffee a couple times a week, when Melanie wasn't working at Ravenswood Nursery. They talked on the phone when there wasn't time to get together.

"What do you think?" asked Gina.

"I think you can't decide what to bring," said Melanie.

"I know. Sad. I'm sixty-five. You'd think I'd be able to figure out life by now."

"Oh, the mind does drift away with you old folks, doesn't it."

"Just you wait, you're only a couple of years behind me," said Gina. She walked into the kitchen and picked up her mug of now cold black tea and sipped it. It was too strong. She would have added more cream, but had used up the last of it. She opened the cupboard and pulled out a water bottle

"So, he said it was casual..."

"I pulled out jeans and t-shirts. And some capris for if it's warm enough. And two pairs of dressier pants and tops."

"You'll be fine. Phone charger?"

"Oh geez." Gina set the water bottle down by the sink and pulled the charger out of the wall above her wood counter top. She walked into the bedroom and put it beneath the suitcase lid. Out of sight from cats.

"My work is done."

"Thanks Melanie." She sat on the bed and petted the cats, who began to purr.

"What time do you want me to pick you up?"

"He's picking me up at the dock at three, so I guess two?"

"Sounds good. I'll leave work early then."

"Are you sure this isn't an imposition?"

"I love leaving work early at this time of year. My feet hurt. I don't know how many more years I can do this."

"I sure couldn't. Last year nearly did me in."

Gina was referring to the incident at Ravenswood Nursery last year when both owners were murdered within a few days of each other, during an important plant conference. The nursery had been part of four days worth of garden tours for the conference. Attendees had come from all over the world. Gina had been dragged in to help with the crowds. The long hours would have been grueling even without the stress of two people being murdered.

Melanie said, "Well, nothing like that going on this year, thank goodness. Just the usual spring rush. But I'm tired of talking to strangers."

"Guess I can't talk you into coming along then. He said there are plenty of open rooms. The wedding's not till the weekend," said Gina.

"Nope. I'm not into hobnobbing with the rich. And tomorrow's my day off. I get to go hang with my granddaughter."

"Definitely beats hanging with strangers."

"Yep. Okay, see you at two. Bye."

"Bye."

Gina went back to the living room and tucked the phone into her brown purse, which she set down on the coffee table by the painting. If she piled everything in the same place, maybe she'd remember it all. She went to the small mud room and collected her rubber shoes, rain hat and coat. Then remembered to fill the water bottle.

What else had she forgotten?

WEDNESDAY AFTERNOON

At 2:30 p.m., Shelley called.

"Hi Mom."

"Hi. Is everything okay?" asked Gina. Her daughter wouldn't have called now unless there was a problem.

"Yeah. My flight just got in at Vancouver. I'm taking the bus down to the outlet mall and I'll catch a cab from there to the island," said Shelley.

"That sounds like a really long day. Will that work for you?"

"I'm feeling rummy already. The flight from Delhi was about fourteen hours. I'll be okay. There's coffee here at the airport and I'll get another one at the outlet mall."

"Okay. You've got the key, right?"

"Right here on my key chain."

"And you've got Melanie's number if you have any problems. The kitchen's stocked up. There's an extra car key on the bulletin board in the kitchen. And the cats are sleeping. Don't let them out. I'll feed them before I go."

"Awesome. I'll see you when you get back. Today's Monday, so that's Thursday night. Or Friday morning," said Shelley, as if checking herself about what day it was.

"Yes."

"You can stay longer if you want, you know. Maybe you'll fall in love with the rich guy."

"Honey, he's married. This is business. I'm placing a painting I did for him and his wife. And what did I teach you about business?"

"Don't shit where you eat?" asked Shelley.

"Exactly. I don't think I'll stay longer. Their daughter's wedding is on Saturday. It will be chaos, I assume."

"Okay, well I'm taking you up on your offer of staying with you for a while, so you can if you want. I need to get my bearings before I leap back into work."

"Good for you. Okay, I'll see you on Thursday night, probably."

It would depend on the weather. The only way onto the private island was by boat. Private boat.

Her rambling daughter had finally returned for a while. Her other daughters were, most likely, permanently settled in L.A. and Boston. But Shelley liked to work her tail off and earn as much money as possible, then wander the world until she ran out of money and return to working. She lived to travel.

Melanie arrived just before two. By that time, Gina had managed to wrangle the cats out of her suitcase by putting down fresh cat food. She was packed and had checked her list of what to bring three times.

She wasn't used to traveling anymore. Ever. She hadn't

gone anywhere for over a decade. At least she wasn't flying, with all the new rules. Which as far as she could tell, hadn't done anything except make traveling harder for everyone.

They loaded up Melanie's car. Then Gina came back in and said goodbye to the cats, who'd taken their respective places, Alice on the back of the couch watching birds out the window and Albert on the easy chair, bathing. Completely ignoring Gina. The silent treatment.

"You two be good. Shelly will be here in a while. I'll be back in a few days." She petted and cuddled them. Then locked the door.

The drive to Everett took only forty-five minutes. There was no traffic at this time of day.

By the time they pulled into park at the marina, and hauled all of Gina's things over to the gate near the pier, Paul Frost was waiting for her. The smell of salt and kelp filled the fresh air.

Paul wore khaki pants, a blue button-up shirt and navy deck shoes. He was medium height and athletic looking for a man in his forties. His blond hair shot through with silver and beginning to thin. He wore sunglasses which looked like they were prescription. Gina had remembered him wearing glasses when they'd met at the gallery opening.

He stood on the metal walkway, the entry gate of chain metal unlocked and open. The walkway passed over a moat of seawater that surrounded the floating docks where people's boats were tied up. A gray and brown spotted harbor seal swam along the surface of the moat, looking around.

"Let me take those," Paul said, taking the box with the painting by its wooden handle and her rolling suitcase. That left Gina with her purse and Melanie with the art bag.

They followed him down the walkway and the gate clanked closed behind them, locking itself automatically. Keeping the peasants out, Gina supposed.

They walked along the floating concrete pier, boats of all kinds docked next to each other. Sailboats next to boats with motors. They walked to the far end of the pier. A two-story, large white boat was tied up on the open end of the pier. Gina didn't know much about boats. This one looked big and safe. Not made for speed, but for luxury. A yacht, that's what boats like that were called. The name painted on the side was *Maggie*. Named after his wife.

Paul set her suitcase down on the pier and walked across a metal gangplank with the boxed painting. The back of the boat was flat and open. You could step right off it and into the water.

Paul ran up a short set of stairs and behind a white partition, then returned empty-handed for the suitcase.

Melanie handed Gina her bag of art supplies and said, "Have a great time. Call me an hour before you want me to pick you up."

"I'll do that," said Gina. "Thanks."

She gave Melanie a hug and nervously walked over the short gangplank. Then onto the rubber looking surface on the back of the boat.

She followed Paul up the short set of stairs, hanging onto the metal handrails. The stair opened up onto a covered area with plastic windows which felt warmed by its protection from the wind. She hadn't even noticed there was a breeze.

Gina went through the open door and walked into what looked like a very cozy living room. All of the plastic and wood were a warm russet brown color in stark contrast to the whiteness outside of the boat.

"Set your things down anywhere," he gestured. He'd put the painting box and suitcase on the floor against the wall. Gina set her art supplies next to the couch and her purse on the couch.

He opened a cupboard and handed her a yellow lifejacket and she put it on. He also put one on.

"Ready?" he asked.

"Yes."

"Have you been on boats before much."

"Just ferries."

"Well, the *Maggie* is a lovely old gal. She rides nice and smooth. I haven't used her a lot, she's on the small side for ocean cruising. But she'll be perfect for ferrying over the wedding guests."

"She's lovely."

"I'll just go get Tom to pull up the gangplank and untie, then we're off."

"Who's Tom?"

"He's the only permanent crew member of the *Maggie*. Chief electrician, pilot, cook and bottle washer. He does everything and lives on the boat. Loves her like she was his very own.

Gina watched through the windows as Paul, and another man, gangly, and gnarled like a piece of weathered wood, untied the boat. Tom jumped on the back of the boat with a grace she wouldn't have been able to copy.

It only took a few minutes to weave their way through the docking area of the marina, past Jetty Island and out onto the choppy waters of Puget Sound.

Gina sat beside Paul in the cockpit, or whatever it was called. It was decorated in the same russet wood and plastic as the living room. It would have been called a living room in a house. What boat people called it, she had no idea. The cockpit had two swiveling chairs. Paul sat in the one closest to most of the controls and pointed out various landmarks. The boat was quite lovely and probably cost more than her house.

"What's down below?" she asked.

"Oh, there's three bedrooms and bathrooms. The engine room. And the crew quarters. I'd forgotten how much I love this boat. I spend more time on our larger one, the *Emma*."

"Named after?" she asked.

"Our daughter. She and her mother are like two peas in a pod. Well almost." He laughed. "I was thinking, do you ever do botanical paintings of sea plants? Kelp?"

"I never have," she said.

"But could you?"

"I don't see why not. I'd have to study them. Why?"

He grinned at her. "I think they'd be perfect for the salon. Between the windows over the couch. And another over the chair on the other side."

"I'll think about it. That might be fun. I don't know much about seaweed."

It took about an hour to get to Frost Island. There were a lot of boats out on the water. Gina never gave much thought to how many people in the area were avid boaters. Even though she lived on an island. It just wasn't her thing.

The docking area was in a small bay. The pier on the island was made of treated wood. The *Maggie* parked in one slot, the much, much larger *Emma* parked in another. A small power boat was tied up on the other side of the dock from the *Maggie*. There were two empty slots, presumably for guests.

Gina could see the house, situated at a high spot on the island. It was huge as she'd expected. One story and rustic wood, but clean, modern lines and plenty of glass.

Tom and Paul loaded her things into a small white SUV and Paul drove her up the hill. Tom stayed behind to tend to the boat.

The paved road up to the house passed by several quaint little cottages, all painted white but each with different colored trim. They were obviously built in a different era than the house, which was much more modern. Paul pointed out the ones occupied by the gardener, and the cook, and the mechanic/handyman, and the housekeeper. That left seven others empty for guests. The house itself had twenty guest rooms, he told her.

Surrounding the cottages and the house was what looked like an extraordinary garden. Some sections were well-maintained lawn bordered by old specimen trees, all of them short. The tall trees like cedars and big leaf maples were kept in the lower parts of the island. Probably where their growth wouldn't block the view from the house. Other sections of the garden looked like complex borders of shrubs, more short trees and smaller flowering plants.

"I can see I'm going to enjoy exploring your gardens," she said.

"Well, somebody should. The wedding guests probably won't. Bunch of New Yorkers. Love the city. They think nothing exists outside of it."

"The bride's side or the groom's?" she asked.

"Both. My family is as close-minded as the groom's. It's

Maggie's family, what few there are of them, who are the nature lovers. The other lot, all they think about is work. Maggie taught me better," he grinned at her.

"You must love her very much."

"I do. I really do, even after all this time."

The circular driveway rounded at a modest two-car garage. Then again, there probably wasn't much need for many cars on the island.

Paul stopped in front of the garage and parked.

As Gina got out of the car, the front door opened and a dark-haired slender woman dressed all in turquoise came out. She wore a tank top with a flowing scarf around her neck, capris and sandals. And an astonishing amount of large-sized jewelry, all turquoise.

She was followed by a tanned muscular middle-aged man. He wore sand-colored slacks, running shoes and a white polo shirt.

The woman came to greet her, while the man went around to the back of the car to help with the luggage.

"Hi. I'm Maggie. You must be Georgina."

"Call me Gina, please." she said, as Maggie engulfed her with a hug.

"Come on in and I'll show you your room. We were about to have Martin here make daiquiris." She gestured to the man carrying Gina's suitcase and art bag.

He nodded at Gina and said, "Pleased to meet you Ms. Wetherby."

Maggie continued, "Martin is our House Manager. Which means he's our butler and much much more. He does everything and knows everything. Better than Siri." Maggie laughed.

Gina tried not to let her mouth drop open. Butlers still existed? This was a world vastly different than hers. No wonder Melanie hadn't wanted to come along.

Maggie had taken her arm and led Gina inside and down a long hallway of taupe-colored wood paneling. Columns of two feet in diameter carved tree trunks served as the support posts for the ceiling. In between the posts stood pedestals topped with statues of all types. One might be a bronze of a cowboy on his horse, the next a marble study of a naked woman, followed by a carved jade dragon. It was like walking through an art gallery without a theme. She supposed the theme was that someone had liked all the statues.

The brown-tiled floor was shiny and reflected the skylights above. The entire entryway gave a feeling of wealth and abundance expressed in a rustic setting.

Maggie pointed to the left. "Down that hallway are the common areas of the house. The house is laid out in a sunray pattern. Here's the center," she said, as they came to a central domed glass room. It was alternately ringed with window seats and hallway entrances.

"Down that hallway are the family bedrooms." Maggie pointed to a hallway with rust-colored tile. "Those two hallways are guest bedrooms."

One had cream-colored tile, the other was directly across from the entrance hallway and the brown tiles continued along it. Each ray passed through the dome and the tile color continued across into the hallway opposite. The cream-colored guest room corridor was directly across from the common rooms.

"So what's down there?" asked Gina, pointing to the rust-tiled hallway that was opposite the family rooms.

"Oh, those are the offices of our staff. That's where all the work actually gets done."

Maggie led her down a brown-tiled hallway and opened a door about halfway down.

Inside was a suite of rooms which felt larger than Gina's house. It overlooked a cottage garden in full bloom. The floor was covered in strips of golden bamboo that resembled hardwood flooring. The room had a high ceiling and one wall of floor to ceiling windows with wooden blinds that could be pulled to cover them completely. All the furniture was made of logs or slabs of smooth varnished wood. Tables were glass and wood. The fabrics were either rich, shiny and silklike, or velvet. The colors in the room were warm burgundies, deep golden browns and deep leaf green.

"Oh, this is beautiful," said Gina.

"I'm so glad you like it," said Maggie. "I thought you'd appreciate the garden view, more than most people anyway."

"I can't wait to wander around the gardens."

"It will take you days." Maggie's smile gleamed with a mischievous tinge.

"Well, I can't stand around placing a painting for days, can I?"

Maggie laughed.

Martin had followed them in carrying Gina's belongings.

"I'll go to the parlor and make those daiquiris," he said, bowing slightly and then left.

Maggie said, "I'll go hunt down Emma and Tristan. Meet you in the parlor in half an hour? After daiquiris we can go for a walk outside."

"Lovely."

"Follow the cream tiles to where all the noise is," said Maggie and left, closing the door behind her.

Gina found that Martin had put her suitcase up on a bench in the bedroom. All she had to do was open it and take the clothes out, putting them in the closet or the dresser. She set her bag of toiletries in the spacious bathroom, noting the large jetted tub.

Next to the king-sized bed, on a nightstand, sat a bouquet of light purple, white and dark purple lilacs. They perfumed the entire room.

The layout of the main room in the suite was such that it angled the bedroom and bathroom in a peculiar way. The bedroom and the living room had huge walls of windows that formed a door and could be covered with the wooden blinds. The windows looked out on more of the gardens, but outside, there were metal screens and thick evergreen shrubs planted in such a way that it was impossible to see into the next room from hers.

After unpacking, she went towards the parlor.

Gina could indeed just follow the noise. The white tiled hallway was hung with paintings of many different styles and mediums. She passed a dining room on the left. It held a large table with a lilac-colored tablecloth on it and dinner settings arranged. Sixteen wooden chairs sat around the table. One end was empty of place settings, although it was covered with the tablecloth.

There were three small vases, with lovely flower arrangements in them, set equally down the table. She spotted lilacs, white foxgloves, bleeding hearts and sprays of salal and another foliage plant she didn't recognize immediately. Evergreen blueberry leaves perhaps?

On the wall, hung two of her paintings. Paul had bought them at the gallery show last spring. Had it really only been a year since that first show? So much had happened since then.

Continuing down the hallway, on the other side she passed a room filled with couches and a large screen tv. Then there was another room with scattered smaller tables that seated four. Perhaps that was a game room. They must entertain a lot.

The last room on her right was the parlor. The walls were a delicate peach color. A generous carved wooden bar, which Martin stood behind, curved around one corner of the room. A large bookcase took up an entire wall and a fireplace another. It was a warm comfortable looking room.

Plush brown leather couches and chairs were grouped around coffee tables. Most of the people were seated at one end. Maggie, Paul and four other people, all younger. One girl sat on the arm of the couch draped over a boy. Well, maybe she was a woman and he was a man, but they looked so very young.

Gina walked in and Martin approached her with a tray that held several daiquiris.

"Would you care for a daiquiri Ms. Wetherby? The red one is strawberry, the green is lime and the yellow is banana."

"Oh, thank you," said Gina, taking the strawberry.

She sipped it, tasting the strong berry flavor.

"Is this made with real berries?" she asked.

"Absolutely," he smiled. "Unfortunately they are from California at this time of year, but fresh berries are the only way."

"Wonderful." Martin was definitely a perfectionist when it came to food.

"Thank you."

Martin returned to the wooden bar in the corner.

She crunched on the grainy ice, her mouth freezing. The rum tasted strong, but didn't overwhelm the strawberries.

"Gina, you made it. Come on in and sit down. I'll do introductions," said Maggie, patting the seat of the couch next to her.

Gina walked over and sat down on the nicely firm couch. Relieved she wouldn't have to fight her way out of it to get up.

Maggie introduced the draping girl as her daughter, Emma, whose blond and blue streaked hair was thick and reached past the middle of her back. Emma's eyes were startlingly blue and she wore a royal blue t-shirt and white shorts. Her long tanned legs ended in delicate feet with blue toenails that peeked through white sandal straps. She looked slender and athletic.

The boy was Tristan. Also blond with blue eyes. He wore a green t-shirt, khaki shorts and sandals. He had a nice smile, but there was something about his demeanor that Gina didn't like. Somehow, he gave off a feeling of snobbishness and sleaziness all at the same time.

The next woman was Maggie's younger sister, Jennifer. She was as voluptuous as Maggie was slender. Jennifer had long red hair, so red it was obviously from a bottle. She wore heavy makeup and a flowing sundress with a gaudy jungle print. She had the same vivacious spirit as Maggie did. Between the two of them, they would be the life of any party.

The last woman was a friend of Jennifer's, Marsha. Marsha was much more subdued. She wore a black tank top and khaki pants along with hiking sandals. She had short brown hair that hung over her lovely hazel eyes. Her laugh was almost musical. Gina liked both her and Jennifer immediately. They seemed so easy going. She suspected the two of them were a couple, but nothing was mentioned to indicate it.

The discussion was mostly about the upcoming wedding. Emma didn't seem to be nervous. Then again, it seemed like Maggie and Jennifer were doing the bulk of the planning. As well as Martin, who stood by the bar the entire time. Gina felt sure he was doing most of the actual work.

Emma asked, "When is everyone arriving again?"

Maggie said, "Mom, Grandma and Elizabeth are coming tomorrow. Then on Friday, all of Paul's family will descend on us. Friday afternoon, Tristan's family is coming. I expect most of your friends will be coming on Saturday afternoon. The last time the boat is coming over is noon. I think that's the one they RSVP'd for."

"What if they didn't RSVP?" asked Emma.

"Then they'll miss the boat. There's only so many people it can carry at a time. They've had two months. And I told them there was a limit so they needed to get their reservations in or miss the wedding. Unless they're coming over on their own boats."

Emma heaved a deep dramatic sigh. "I know Karyn didn't reply. She can't plan that far ahead."

"Well then, text her and tell her what time to show up. The 10 a.m. boat still has two spaces left," said Maggie.

"And everything else is on track?"

"Tiffany has hired a couple of cooks from off-island; people she worked with at her last job. They're already here and hard at work. She's baking the cake on Thursday and decorating it on Saturday morning. The other two women will handle everything else, with her supervision, so you know it will all taste and look fabulous. The groceries are all here. Dustin is going to begin picking the flowers on Friday morning. The florist will come Thursday afternoon and decide what to use. There's lots to choose from. She's bringing over some greenhouse flowers, too. Gardenias for corsages and I don't know what all," said Maggie. "And the rehearsal dinner is Friday night. Just after the rehearsal."

"So, it's all on track," said Emma.

"Yes. So stop worrying."

"Isn't that what brides are supposed to do?"

"I don't know," said Maggie. "Paul and I eloped. He didn't want to have to deal with his family. I didn't want to have to deal with mine either. It was so much simpler. And a bit dangerous," said Maggie, slyly.

Paul laughed and patted her knee.

"And the rooms are ready for all those people who are staying here?" asked Emma.

"What do you think?" asked Maggie.

"Of course they are," said Emma.

The daiquiris finished, people drifted off. Emma and Tristan to play tennis before dinner. Jennifer and Marsha for naps. They'd been traveling for most of the day and were tired. Paul went to deal with some business matter.

Maggie and Gina headed off for the garden.

The sun was lower in the sky and the wind off the water made the heat of the day cool down somewhat. Not that April was ever too hot. Still, Gina felt glad of her sweater.

The garden was laid out in rooms. Each one defined by the doorway that opened out in the center of it. There was a stunning tropical room right off the pool. In the summer it would be filled with large-leafed plants: *Gunnera*, bananas and

Canna lilies. Now, those plants were just barely breaking the ground, if that.

"We haven't brought the containers out of the greenhouse yet," said Maggie. "It's still too cool. Maybe by the middle of May."

The area still looked beautiful, filled with spring bulbs: orange, red and yellow tulips, salmon-colored *Narcissus* and purple *Alliums*. The garden looked bright and gaudy, as a tropical garden should be. There were *Begonias* with fancy leaves and many spring annuals tucked in.

"Angus has done a wonderful job of making sure this garden has some zing right now. It's not usually quite this colorful, but he wanted everything to be perfect for the wedding."

"It's got so much color. A tough thing to do this early in the season. Does he grow all the plants or have them brought in?"

"He grew most of them, although I know he's taken a couple of trips to the mainland and brought back a lot of plants. Paul kept complaining about Angus and his messy plants on the boat."

"How did he shop? Does he have a car on the other side?"

"Paul keeps a pickup on the other side. So he can run and buy things that are needed. Then they haul it over on the *Maggie*. Or if it's really large, the *Emma*." She laughed. "One time they hauled over a jetted tub. It was pretty funny to watch them unload it."

They walked around the tip of one ray of the building and over to the greenhouse. Inside it was steamy and warm. The scents were amazing. Jasmine climbed up one section. Gina noticed it was planted right into the soil. A permanent plant. Fragrant roses in large containers were in full bloom. This wasn't just a working greenhouse, it was an elegant glasshouse. There were wrought iron chairs and tables, white wicker table sets and even a huge pond in the center.

Gina looked down into the huge pond. The koi were massive. Larger than she'd ever seen. There were only seven of them, but each was easily three to four feet long and a couple of feet deep. They swam to the surface when she and Maggie came to the side of the pond, mouths open.

"Bunch of beggars," said Maggie. "They're inside so they get to eat all winter long. And it's warm in here at this time of year, so they're really hungry. All the time. I think Angus feeds them three times a day.

Maggie picked up a plastic container and threw in a couple handfuls of food. The koi sucked it down, swirling through the water in streaks of orange, white, black and yellow.

The greenhouse was filled with exotic tropical plants. Palm trees, Tasmanian tree ferns and citrus trees just coming into bloom.

One large section of the wall held passion flower plants, or maybe it was all one plant. Gina had only seen blue and white ones before, but this one was pink with white tinges around the edges of the petals and white stigmas or anthers. Or maybe the white was part of the petals. The stigmas and anthers looked like they should belong to a spinning top. She should know which was which and had at one time. The center of the flower was a deep brown mass which stuck out about half an inch. The sexual parts protruded a good inch.

Passion flowers were the most amazing things. They looked like they'd come from another planet, even though they were quite lovely. En masse the scent was sweet and powerful. The vines had curly tendrils that had latched onto the metal framework of the glasshouse. It too was planted into the soil. The vines were putting on a spectacular show.

She'd have to come back and paint them.

"All of the containers will be taken out near the pool once it's warm enough," said Maggie. "That makes the garden so exotic in the summer."

They were just about ready to leave the greenhouse when a loud gonging sound echoed through the area.

"Dinner," said Maggie, grinning. "I wonder what Tiffany has dreamed up for tonight. She's such an inventive cook. Makes me never want to travel."

WEDNESDAY EVENING

Gina followed Maggie out a side door of the glass house and down a narrow gravel path through a maze of tall *Camellia*. Ahead, Gina could see the tip of the closest ray of the building.

As they approached, she recognized the circular driveway off to their right. This was the main entrance. This garden was very confusing. Lots of main walkways and many more paths which were mostly hidden. Maggie opened the front door and they were inside, walking the length of the entry hall to the dome and then taking a left down the cream-colored tiles to the common rooms and the dining room.

Everyone else was already there. Maggie sat across from Gina. Paul was at one end, Emma at the other. Jennifer was on Gina's right, Tristan on Gina's left. Marsha next to Maggie.

Gina unfolded her linen napkin and set it on her lap, beneath the edge of the lavender tablecloth.

"How was your walk around the garden?" asked Jennifer,

unfolding her napkin with a flourish and arranging it in her lap.

"Short. We didn't get very far."

"I'm not into plants myself. They're pretty. I suppose if I had a gardener I'd have some, but they're not worth the effort for me. I've killed all my houseplants. I'm just gone too much of the time."

"What do you do with your time?" asked Gina.

"I work for Caviar Cruises, down in San Francisco. We specialize in luxury cruises to exotic places, so I get to travel. And bring Marsha with me most times."

"Oh, that sounds fun. What do you do?"

"I'm the Marketing Director."

"So you do all the ad campaigns?"

"I oversee the folks who do. Basically I get to tell people what to do. And encourage them to be creative, while not thinking too far outside the box. Our clients tend to be rather conservative."

"Perfect job for you, my bossy sister," said Maggie.

"Well if you would just do what I suggested the first time around, I wouldn't have to be so bossy," said Jennifer, sticking her tongue out at her sister.

Gina laughed.

Three slender young women in white aprons walked in carrying large trays, containing clear glass plates with green salads. They set the salad plates down on top of the lavender dinner plates, putting one in front of each person.

"Thank you," said Gina.

Martin followed the women into the room and put down three baskets of steaming hot bread slices at different spots along the center of the long table, next to plates of butter pats.

The salad contained wild greens, dried cranberries, a soft goat cheese and a tangy dressing of balsamic vinegar, poppy seeds and olive oil. There were hazelnuts on the side to sprinkle over it, which Gina did.

She took a bite of the salad and the flavors exploded in her mouth. She tasted mustard greens, arugula and another flavor, almost licorice. The cranberries and roasted hazelnuts formed a sweet contrast to the dressing. The goat cheese added a roundness to the flavor, a richness which let everything meld together. It all tasted superb.

The next course was steak grilled to perfection. The smoky flavor mingled well with the beefy taste of the tender meat and Martin served a local red wine which completed the course.

She was hoping there were only two courses. By the time Gina finished her steak she felt stuffed.

Luckily, the only thing after that was a wine glass filled with chocolate mousse. The texture was light and fluffy, in contrast to the strong intense chocolate. Gina could gain a lot of weight if she lived here.

After dinner there was a choice of coffee, tea or port. She chose mint tea. Maybe it would help her digest all the food. She probably shouldn't have eaten that entire large piece of steak, but it tasted so delicious.

Most of the others had coffee. Only Tristan had port.

Paul said, "Not tonight. I've got some work to finish up." He chose coffee, too.

The talk during dinner had been mostly about relatives and the upcoming wedding. Gina felt slightly out of place since she knew none of the people being talked about. Marsha also didn't join in the conversation. Gina wasn't sure if that was because the woman was normally quiet, or if she didn't know them either. How long had Marsha and Jennifer been a couple?

Tristan knew all of the people, or at least he had an opinion on them. Then again he seemed to be one of those people who have an opinion on everything and think that everyone wanted to hear their opinion. Gina knew she was being petty, but she disliked the boy. And she really didn't want to hear what he thought about the people who were about to become his relatives.

Emma seemed to be a bit on the spoiled side. Or maybe it was pre-wedding jitters bringing out the worst in her. She kept asking the same questions again and again. As if she wasn't really listening to the answers.

Gina remembered her wedding and how nervous she'd been. Oh, how she missed Ewan sometimes. He would have had something to say about Tristan. Then again if he was still alive, she probably wouldn't be here.

After dinner, she went back to her room and checked messages. She called Shelly and they talked for a while. Gina felt relieved her daughter had made it to her house safe and sound. It sounded like the latest trip was both harrowing and invigorating, giving her daughter a new sense of direction in life. Shelly promised details and photos when Gina returned home.

There were still three hours of good light left. Gina put on a sweater and took herself out into the garden again. A different section this time. There was a sunny border filled with roses that were beginning to bud up, but it would be another month or so before they bloomed. Hardy *Geranium* were blooming. The small flowers littering the beds in pale pink and bright fuchsia pink. Tall purple and white monkshood and pink and white foxgloves shot upwards like exclamation marks among the shorter perennials. Flowering *Viburnum* with pinkish-white, sweetly-scented blossoms formed the backbone of this garden. Gina could see *Clematis* vines snaking through the shrubs, readying themselves for their own show.

She was lost in the scent of moist soil, the scent of sweet *Daphne* and a fresh salty-smelling breeze off the Sound. This garden was delightful. Small bushtits flitted through the nearby shrubs. There was a lamb's ear nearby and she reached down to touch the velvety leaves. A sleek black cat stalked the birds, when Gina looked at it the cat melted into the shrubbery and vanished.

Gina continued on around what seemed to be the main path. The next garden was all in shade. *Arisaema* were abundant. Their exotic jack-in-the pulpit flowers in shades of black-purple, white or green, solid and striped, mingled with many species of ferns, fawn lilies and other collector's plants.

She stood staring at a stunning Mayapple with large green leaves spotted with dark purple in a particularly amazing pattern. This garden was jaw-dropping. Everywhere she turned was a well-thought-out arrangement. She had to paint some of these plants.

She'd circled around one ray of the house, barely able to see the roofline behind the tall shrubs and trees. Where was she? She needed to find this section again tomorrow.

Gina heard a loud scream. She ran in the direction the sound was coming from and found herself in a garden outside one of the bedrooms, similar to the courtyard outside her window.

The large windows formed a door, which stood wide open.

Gina ran inside to find a short young woman in black pants and t-shirt and wearing a white apron. She carried a stack of bath towels. The woman stood in the middle of a sitting room, screaming. Tristan lay at her feet, pale and unmoving.

"Call 911," said Gina.

The woman looked at her for a moment, then set the towels on a table and left. Running down the hall yelling, "Mr. Frost. Mrs. Frost."

Gina tried to find Tristan's pulse, but there wasn't one. His skin felt cold. What had happened? It couldn't have been long.

It had been about half an hour since she'd left the dinner table to wander the gardens. Tristan had still been at the table when she left.

Paul came running in and said, "What happened Gayle?"

The woman ran in after him. "I came to bring his towels. He didn't answer. So I let myself in and found him here like this."

"No one else was here?" he asked.

"No. Ms. Wetherby came in from the garden and said *Call 911.* So I called you. I didn't know if 911 would work for us out here on the island."

Paul checked for a pulse and found none.

Paul took a phone out of his slacks pocket and punched in a number. They kept him on the line for quite a while. At the same time, he texted Martin. The phone buzzed as the text was sent.

"Martin knows some first aid. I don't."

The smell of vomit was strong in the room. Gina glanced in the bedroom and saw where Tristan had thrown up.

She looked around and noticed a glass of wine on a side table. Along with a carafe that was half full. Or was it more of the port he'd had after dinner? Everything else in the rooms looked clean and tidy. Except for the towels the maid had brought in, there was nothing out of place. She couldn't see a wound. Had Tristan been poisoned?

Who would do such a thing?

Finally, Paul hung up and said, "They're sending a helicopter with medics."

He closed the door to the hallway.

"Don't tell Emma. Don't tell anyone. Not till they get here and we know what's happened."

"Should you call the police?" Gina asked.

"We'll let the medics come first. Maybe he's had a heart attack or something."

"Do you know if he has a history of heart problems or illness?" asked Gina.

"I don't know," said Paul. His face wrinkled up with worry. "How am I going to tell Emma?"

"I don't know," said Gina.

"Mr. Frost, should I go back to work?"

"Not just yet, Gayle. Work will still be there tomorrow. I'll tell Sheila that I need your help with a guest problem for the time being."

He typed in a text and the phone buzzed as it was sent off.

"I need to sit down," he said, looking around.

"If this is a crime scene, the police won't like it. Maybe we should go and sit out on the patio."

He nodded and the three of them went out the open glass door and sat at the cafe table. The chairs were made of some sort of plastic webbing and would have been comfortable if one wasn't thinking about the dead body in the next room. Gina couldn't see inside what with all the shrubbery.

Maybe Tristan had fainted. No, one of them would have found a pulse. The man hadn't been breathing. There were no signs of life.

Still, Gina kept thinking she should go back in. Perform CPR or at least pretend to. What if he had something stuck in his throat?

"Sit. There's nothing we can do except wait," said Paul. Then picked up his phone and read something. He responded with another text.

"Martin tried CPR, with no luck. He's going to take the SUV over to the airfield to wait for the helicopter and bring the medics."

It seemed to take forever for the helicopter to fly over the house and land. Tense moments of the three of them staring at each other. Gayle was crying and shaking. Gina put her arm around the young woman's shoulders and the maid relaxed against her, willing to take comfort from a complete stranger.

Finally, Gina could hear the medics and Martin in the sitting room. Paul went inside and talked to them about what happened.

Gina rose to her feet and could see in through the open doorway. The medics did an exam and then stood up. Gina could tell from the way the one raised his hands while talking to Paul that there was nothing they could do.

The medics joined Gina and Gayle at the table, as Paul called the sheriff. Gina figured the medics would probably take Tristan's body back with them, or maybe they needed to be here when the sheriff came. She didn't know exactly how things worked.

Martin left, then returned with coffee and chocolate chip cookies.

"Does Maggie know what's happened?" asked Paul.

Martin said, "No one does. Emma is in her room talking to friends on her phone. Maggie is watching a movie with Jennifer and Marsha. The other staff are also occupied."

Martin obviously didn't miss a thing.

"Thank you. I'd like to keep this quiet until we actually know what's happened. And keep everyone away from here, especially Emma."

"Very good sir."

Martin poured coffee and left.

Gina sipped a cup of dark bitter coffee and poured some cream into it. She didn't normally drink coffee, but once it had been a necessary part of her life. An addiction. She savored the richness, wishing there was a shot of whiskey to put in it. Somehow, that seemed like it would be a comfort right now. She hadn't particularly liked Tristan, but she still felt sadness for him. And poor Emma, to lose her fiancé just days before the wedding.

Paul seemed like one of those people who hid their emotions fairly well. He was quiet, except when the medics asked a question. But his fingers nervously drummed on the table and his face looked pinched, as if he was holding back.

Gayle was a mess. Poor girl, she looked not much older than college age. She couldn't seem to stop crying. The girl just sat there, tears leaking from her eyes, as soon as she brushed the previous ones away. She was probably in shock from finding a dead body. Had the girl known Tristan? She mentioned his name when talking about delivering the towels. Had Tristan been a frequent guest? Did Emma normally live here or did she have another home?

Paul finally went and got her a box of tissues. Gayle began making quite a pile of used ones. She must be quite a sensitive soul and was so young that she'd probably never seen a dead body. Gina grew anxious and impatient for the sheriff to arrive.

What was she doing here, anyway? She'd come to deliver the painting. To see what other paintings Paul and Maggie wanted done. And they'd insisted she come to see the spring garden and find plants to paint for them.

Gina *hadn't* come to see another murder. And another investigation. She didn't want to go through all that again, but knew her mind wouldn't be able to let the puzzle go. Sometimes she hated the part of her brain that couldn't just let go of things. It was like a bulldog.

So she better just give in and figure it out.

Who would want to kill Tristan? And why?

There couldn't be that many people on the island. There were the household staff and guests. That's all she knew about.

"Are there any families who live on the island?" she asked Paul.

He looked at her, bewildered for several seconds, then said, "No. Just us. The only people who are here are my family, our guests and the staff. That's it. Why?"

"Just curious. I've never been to a private island before. I wondered how it worked. You've no doctor, no police, no post office."

"There's not that much mail. We have a post office box in Everett. Most everything is done online these days."

"Where does your electricity come from?"

"We create it ourselves. Every building is covered with solar panels. And on the other side of the island is a wind farm. Not a large one, but it's enough."

"And water?"

"We have a deep well."

"Fascinating," said Gina.

One of the medics said, "My brother has solar panels on his house. Gets enough energy from them that he sells it back to PUD. Makes a tidy sum there."

Just then Paul's phone rang. He stood up and walked away from the table.

"Paul here."

He listened intently for a minute.

"I'll send Martin down with a car."

Then he sent another text.

"Sheriff and deputy are almost here."

"How did they get here?" asked Gina.

"Boat. The sheriff's office has a boat."

"Are you part of Island County?"

"Yes."

Well, that made sense. There were three or maybe four large islands in the county and plenty of shoreline. A boat would come in handy.

Within five minutes the sheriff and deputy were in Tristan's room. Gina was surprised to see it was Sheriff Jansson and Deputy Hammond. But then Raven Island was part of Island County. Were the sheriffs on call and whoever could come, would? Part of the County's budget cuts? Island County was a big place, but Raven Island and Everett and Frost Island were all close to each other. Although Everett was big enough to have its own police force for the city even though it was part of Snohomish County.

Gina kept her mind on petty details, trying to figure things out so she wouldn't become overwhelmed with the awfulness of the situation.

Tristan was dead and Gina felt sure he'd been murdered. He was a healthy young man. If the medics had found a reason for his death and if it hadn't been suspicious, then they wouldn't have had the sheriff called in.

So, it had been murder. Which meant the person who killed him was most likely still on the island. The chances that someone had snuck onto the island, killed Tristan and left were very remote. No, it was most likely someone who was still here. Probably someone who knew him very well. Most people killed for a reason.

But what was it?

The medics went in and spoke to the sheriff. Paul rejoined Gayle and Gina at the table. Martin came out and asked, "Can I get anyone anything?"

Gina shook her head. Gayle didn't answer.

Paul said, "I think that'll be enough, Martin. Just continue to keep tabs on the others. I'll text if we need anything."

The sun was beginning to set and the temperatures were dropping.

"I'll turn on the heater," said Martin.

He must have noticed her shivering even with her sweater on.

Paul went over to one of the large towering heaters and turned it on. Gina was surprised by how quickly she felt the heat coming her way.

"Thank you," she said.

After Martin left, Gina poured herself another cup of coffee. She wouldn't be able to sleep for a long time tonight, anyway. Maybe not at all. Which meant she'd be a walking zombie tomorrow. Well, maybe she'd have coffee in the morning too and catch a nap during the day.

The sheriff and deputy were inside taking photos. Gina could see the flash going off. She'd have to remember to tell him that the door to the garden had been open when she got there. Maybe there were prints on the handle.

"How are you going to deal with all the people coming to the wedding?" asked Gina.

"I don't know. I guess we're going to have to email or text or call them and tell them not to come. Terrible thing to have to tell them Tristan's dead. I'm more worried about how to tell Emma."

"Does she live here or on the mainland?"

"She has a house on Queen Anne. In Seattle, but she's spent a lot of time here in the last several months. Preparing for the wedding."

"How does she get here so often?"

"Mostly, she charters a plane and flies in. Sometimes, she drives up to Everett and I pick her up. Other times, I take the boat to Seattle and pick her up."

"Where did Tristan live?"

"In Seattle. He has a condo there but I think he and Emma lived together, too."

"And his family are coming from back East. And your family too."

"Yes, I'd better get on the phone early tomorrow morning and hope it's not too late to catch them before they begin traveling. Although I guess they'll need to come out for a funeral now. Awful thing to have to tell them." Paul rubbed his face as if that would change everything.

She and Paul talked quietly. Rather, he talked and she listened. Him planning out loud what needed to be done to cancel the wedding. Gayle sat in the chair across from them, quietly weeping. She hadn't really said anything. Gina had tried to comfort her, but there was nothing she could say to the girl. No real comfort she could actually give her.

It seemed to take forever for the sheriff to finish and come out to talk to them.

"Hello," he said to all of them. "I'm Sheriff Jansson. I've met Paul, and I know Ms. Wetherby. Who are you?" he asked Gayle.

"I'm Gayle Monahan. I'm a maid here." Gayle wiped the tears from her face, but more kept coming.

"And you found the body?"

She nodded.

"I'll talk to you first. Paul, is there a place I can go talk to people, alone?"

"I'll open up the next room," Paul said, pointing to the outcropping of the building on the right.

"Perfect," said the Sheriff.

Paul said, "Follow me," and walked around a curving bed of variegated laurels that formed a green and white wall, ten feet high.

The sheriff gestured to Gayle and they left, leaving Gina alone with her coffee. She took out her phone to check her messages and emails. Looking for something comforting, but finding nothing except people wanting to sell her things.

She turned off her phone and sat, staring at the open

garden door to Tristan's room. Forced herself to take a deep breath and think. Who would have wanted to kill him?

She should go through this methodically.

Paul? Maybe he didn't like Tristan. Didn't want him marrying his daughter. If Tristan died from poison, was it in the wine? Or the port from dinner? Paul hadn't had any port and neither had anyone else.

Maggie? Same thing. Maybe she didn't want Tristan to marry Emma. They always said poison was a woman's weapon. Then again, that was from way back when men carried swords and guns. Most men didn't anymore. Gina couldn't come up with another possible motive for Maggie.

Did Tristan have any secrets? Terrible secrets? Secrets that had come out over the length of the engagement?

Could Emma have killed him? They had been together every time Gina had seen them. Why hadn't they been together tonight? Was the bride having second thoughts about marrying? That didn't seem a reason for murder. Unless Tristan had secrets that were worth murdering over.

Gayle? She seemed an unlikely murderer, but she obviously felt very emotional about all this. Did she know Tristan? Her reaction and the length of it seemed like there was something deeper there. Had she seen other dead bodies and seeing Tristan brought something back or was this a reaction to seeing Tristan dead? Had she killed him and the crying was an attempt to look like she wasn't guilty? Or was Gayle just an over-emotional sort of person, young and with no experience of death?

Martin? That cliche, the butler did it, was a cliche for a reason. It seemed unlikely, but maybe he had a thing for

Emma. Maybe Tristan did have a terrible secret and Martin found out. Maybe he had been protecting her.

Then there were Jennifer and Marsha. They also both seemed very, very unlikely as murderers. But they both knew Emma well and perhaps would kill to protect her.

And the housekeeper, the gardener, the cooks, Tom from the boat. And wasn't there a mechanic and handyman who Paul had mentioned? None of them had an obvious reason to kill Tristan.

But if the poison was in the port, then perhaps Tristan wasn't the target. Perhaps Paul was. Hadn't he said, *not tonight. I've got some work to finish up*?

Which meant he often had port after dinner. Often enough to make tonight an exception.

And if Paul was the target that was an entirely different scenario. Any of the people who worked for him might have a reason to kill him. He seemed like a rather nice man, but maybe he was very good at covering up who he really was. Maggie might have a strong reason to kill him. Or maybe even Emma.

Presumably, if Paul was the target, the murderer wasn't Tristan. He wouldn't have poisoned the port and then drank it.

Unless he was trying to commit suicide. Awful way to go though. But who knew what the poison was? Maybe it was faster, or easier, than a shot to the head.

But if the target was Paul, then it could have been anyone on the island. It depended on who he really was. And what someone might have against him. No one at the table had tried to stop Tristan from drinking the port. So, if Paul was the target, then presumably no one at the table who cared for Tristan had been involved. Or maybe the person was all right with Tristan being collateral damage. Or maybe it was someone who wasn't at the table. One of the staff, possibly.

By the time Paul returned to the table and said, "He's ready to talk to you," Gina's brain had become a tangle of what-ifs.

She left the half-finished coffee behind and followed Paul around the laurel hedge to the next room. She went inside through the glass garden door, which Paul closed between them and left.

Inside the sitting room, the lights were all on. Gina squinted at the brightness. The room was entirely white. Furnishing, walls and floor. Every single decoration was white. The only exceptions was a modern painting in the style of Kandinsky. It was mostly white, punctuated by a rainbow of colors in droplets of paint. There was a lot of movement from black lines that streaked through the colors, but it really did nothing for her.

The room smelled slightly stuffy. Sheriff Jansson sat at a round white table and Gina sat down across from him in a white wooden chair.

"Good evening," he said. "I was surprised to see you here."

"I came to deliver a painting. Maggie and Paul have been trying to get me here for months to see their garden. I finally gave in. I was planning on leaving Thursday when Paul went back to Everett to ferry wedding guests over."

"So, you were the second person in the room?"

"Yes, I was out in the garden when I heard a woman, Gayle, scream and I ran in through the open garden door."

"Did you see anyone else in the garden?"

"No. No one."

"Did you know Tristan?"

"I just met him today. There were daiquiris before dinner.

And then I saw him again at dinner. He's a complete stranger to me. Was it poison?"

"Too soon to tell. What makes you think that?"

"Well, after dinner, he was the only one who had port. And in his room I saw a carafe of wine or port, and a half full glass. I didn't see any wound and he was so young. A heart attack didn't seem likely. But I did notice he'd vomited."

The sheriff nodded.

"Did you notice any tension between Tristan and anyone else?"

"No. Tristan didn't seem to feel it necessary to hide his feelings about some of the people, who aren't here yet. Those who were about to become his relatives. I didn't see anyone react badly to his comments. But, I just wanted to add that after dinner Paul said something about the port. He said, *not tonight. I have work to finish up.* Which made me think, a few minutes ago, what if Tristan wasn't the target? What if Paul normally has port. And what if he was the target of the poison?"

"That's interesting. How well do you know these people?"

"Not well at all. We've been emailing back and forth for a year. I met Paul at the gallery opening last year. He bought a painting and commissioned a couple of others. Then commissioned the one I just delivered."

"Have you been in contact with just him, or with his wife?"

"Both. They both seem like very nice slightly eccentric people, but most of our talk has been business."

"So you can't tell me who did it yet?" he asked, smiling slightly.

"You don't need my help."

"No, but it hasn't escaped me that you have a keen sense of

judgement about people and situations. You see things I might miss and people might say things to you that they wouldn't say in my hearing."

"Well I'm sure no one's going to confess murder to me, but I'll keep my ears and eyes open. It would help if you told me if he was poisoned or not."

Sheriff Janssen grinned.

"You know I have to treat you as a suspect just like everyone else."

"I know. I didn't really like the boy, but I had no reason to kill him. I didn't even have enough nerve to tell him to stop abusing his relatives, let alone poison him."

"So you don't have any idea who did it?"

"Like I said, it depends on if he was the target or Paul. If it was Paul, then that widens the field a bit more, doesn't it? But what if Tristan poisoned himself to commit suicide? And perhaps implicate someone else? I think any answer to this has to include finding out if Tristan had any secrets."

"What sort of secrets?" asked the sheriff.

"I don't know. You're the detective, not me. Was he having an affair? Did he owe people money? Was he involved with some sort of crime? I don't know much about him other than what he presented to us over daiquiris and dinner."

"Well, we'll be looking into all that. In the meantime I'm asking everyone to stay here on the island."

"Well, I guess there's not going to be a wedding, so I won't need to vacate my room for guests."

"Not unless the bride comes up with another groom quickly. I don't have any other questions for you right now. I'd appreciate it if you'd keep your eyes and ears open over the next couple of days and let me know if you find anything out."

"Not much else for me to do. Other than take photographs of the garden and maybe paint. I'll need to call my daughter and warn her I won't be coming back home immediately."

"She staying with you?"

"Cat sitting. She's in-between trips. Not the daughter you met last year. This is my traveling daughter."

A wailing came from the hallway and Sheriff Jansson stood and said, "Excuse me."

He went out the hall door, leaving it open.

"Oh my god, why didn't you tell us, Paul?" Maggie yelled at him.

She heard Paul's quiet reply. Gina got up from the table and peered out into the hall.

The medics had Tristan's body on a gurney and around it stood Emma, Maggie, Paul and the sheriff. The medics stood back behind everyone. Gina noticed that Tristan's face was uncovered.

Emma's face looked blanched, but Gina couldn't tell what she was feeling beyond shock. Horror, anger or grief? Or could it be relief? Maggie was crying and flailing about as if she were the betrothed. Then again, she had seemed like a more emotional person. Paul looked frustrated and anxious.

The sheriff began speaking quietly to them. His back was to Gina so she couldn't hear what he said.

She kept watching Emma. The girl didn't shed a tear. Yet, it looked like she'd explode with emotion. Gina just couldn't pin down which one.

When the sheriff stopped talking Emma asked a couple of questions. He answered.

Emma reached out and touched Tristan's hair and then pulled away, shivering. Maggie reached out to embrace her, but Emma just turned and ran down the hall towards the center of the house. She turned into the ray leading to the family's rooms and after a short time, Gina heard a door slam shut.

The medics covered Tristan's face again and wheeled the gurney down the hall towards the main entrance.

The sheriff spoke to Maggie and Paul for a few minutes and then they both walked down the hall to their room. Paul had his arm around Maggie's shoulders as she shuddered with sobs.

The sheriff turned around and Gina walked back to sit at the table. He returned to the room and closed the door.

"Now, where were we?" he asked.

"You were telling me not to leave town."

"Well then, I guess we're done for tonight. You should get some sleep. I'd guess you normally don't stay up this late."

She looked at her watch. It was three in the morning. No wonder she felt so tired.

"You're right. I generally go to bed when the sun goes down. Except in the winter because that's a bit too early."

"I'll see you tomorrow. I might have more questions."

"Hope I have more answers."

She went out the door and walked back towards her own room. Deputy Hammond was at Tristan's door putting up yellow crime scene tape across the door. The woman's brown hair had grown a bit longer, down to her chin, but the tight curls hadn't diminished.

Gina waved at her and the deputy waved back, although Gina wasn't sure the deputy recognized her. Gina walked down the quiet hallway. Had the staff been told about Tristan's death and that the wedding was cancelled? Were they asleep? She wasn't sure what time the cooks got up to start breakfast.

She went down the brown-tiled hallway to her room and opened the door. Her room was quiet and smelled of lilacs. At least that was a comfort. After putting on her soft cotton pajamas and crawling into bed, she was asleep in no time.

THURSDAY MORNING

I t was nine before she woke the next morning.

Gina rushed through the shower and dressed, hoping she could still get some breakfast.

In the dining room, Maggie was the only one there. She looked rumpled, with bags under her eyes and wearing no makeup or jewelry except her wedding ring. It looked like she had just barely brushed her hair. Had the woman even slept? Her eyes were red and puffy as if she'd spent all night crying.

"Good morning," said Gina, out of habit. Then realized it wasn't, couldn't, be a good morning.

Maggie looked up from her cup of coffee as if she'd come out of a trance.

"Morning," she said.

"Am I too late to get some breakfast?"

"Not in this house," said Maggie, gesturing at the sideboard loaded with pastries and steam trays. "If you want eggs over easy, Tiffany will be happy to make you some. Well, maybe happy isn't the right word. I don't think anyone's happy today."

"I know. His death is terrible. And the wedding being cancelled must be a great disappointment to everyone. I didn't see the sideboard. My goodness, this is a feast."

"It is. There's three cooks in the kitchen and the refrigerators are stuffed with food. I told the two cooks who came to help out with the wedding that since they can't leave the island, the least we can do is pay them for their time. So they're doing their best to use up all the food before it spoils."

Gina dished up some scrambled eggs and took two slices of bacon. She set the plate on the table next to Maggie, then went back for a cup of coffee. She'd really need it to wake up this morning. She also needed to get a nap in this afternoon.

The eggs were seasoned with fresh herbs, sharp cheddar cheese, yellow and red bell peppers. She tasted basil and perhaps lemon thyme. The bacon was crisp and not overdone. At least Gina would eat well if she had to remain here.

Maggie said, "I'm sorry to be so out of sorts this morning. I'm not being a very good hostess."

"It's understandable given the circumstances."

"I stayed up half the night emailing my side of the family about the wedding being cancelled. Then at five, I called Tristan's parents, and his other relatives. Since it was eight in the morning where they live, over on the east coast. Most of them are still coming, because they now have a funeral to plan and attend. And since they were traveling today it didn't make sense to change everyone's plane tickets. I told them they're welcome to stay here and have the funeral here if they wish. Although Tristan's body is now in Everett, so I don't know what they'll decide. I feel so awful, as if this is my fault," Maggie said.

Tears began to leak from her eyes.

Gina gave her a hug and asked, "How can it possibly be your fault?"

"It happened at my house. A young man, just a boy still, was poisoned. At my house."

"Did the sheriff say it was poison?"

"Not yet. But they took the wine in his room. And the port from dinner. And asked for food samples. The cooks couldn't give them Tristan's actual dishes. Those were all long cleaned up."

"Well let me ask you this, did you poison him?"

"No," said Maggie, continuing to weep.

"And did you know anyone else was planning to poison him and fail to stop them?"

"No."

"Then I would say it's not your fault. It's the fault of the person who killed him, if he was murdered."

"You don't think he was murdered?" asked Maggie, a hopeful look on her face.

"I'm still hoping for heart attack, or brain aneurism, or some sort of natural cause."

"I suppose that's possible," said Maggie, wiping at her eyes with a linen napkin. "I just assumed that since the sheriff came. ..."

"He had to come, because it was a suspicious death. They won't know anything till a coroner can look at Tristan's body."

"So my sitting her feeling guilty is a waste of energy."

"Yes, and no matter what they find, there's nothing you

could have done to stop a murder you didn't know was happening."

"Thank you," said Maggie. "I have problems getting perspective on things. Usually Paul helps me with that, but he's been so busy. Trying to talk to Emma. Trying to help call people. And just generally holding things together around here."

"How is Emma taking this?"

"I don't really know. She won't talk to me. She's been talking to Jenny, I think. But not me."

"Well, that doesn't help you, does it?"

"No, it makes me feel as if it's my fault. Same with talking to Tristan's relatives."

"Why didn't Paul call them?"

"He was sleeping. He got to bed later than I did, poor thing."

Marsha walked in the door. She wore a tank top, workout shorts and running shoes.

"There's still food out," she said. "Thank goodness, cause I'm famished."

"Lots of it," said Maggie. "The kitchen staffs' response is to feed us all to make us feel better. Plus there's a ton of food that they want to use before it spoils."

"Are any of your other relatives coming?" asked Gina.

"Not most of them, they've cancelled. Which is a relief. I'm fine with you two and Jennifer here. I've always been closest to Jenny."

"How many people are coming from Tristan's family?"

"Ten," said Maggie. "His parents, seven siblings and one spouse."

"Well, none of us can leave, so you'll have plenty of help

entertaining them, provided they stay here."

"I think they will. Just out of curiosity. They'll want to make sure we're okay people and they'll want to know who murdered their son and brother," said Maggie.

Marsha sat down across from Gina and Maggie.

"Would they have the nerve to come here and do that?" asked Marsha.

"I think they would," said Maggie. "Tristan always claimed to be the most meek one in his family. He said everyone else was brazen."

Gina tried not to raise her eyebrows. Tristan had been anything but meek. If he were right though, that didn't bode well for his family taking his death politely.

"Well, I'm not sure you can believe everything Tristan said," said Marsha. "He was very young."

Maggie said nothing, just looked down into her empty coffee cup.

"Have you eaten anything?" asked Gina.

"I'm not sure."

"Let me dish you up some scrambled eggs, they're delicious. And some bacon. And how about a danish? They look wonderful," said Gina.

"All right," said Maggie. "I really should eat. I don't think I've eaten since last night, at dinner. All I've done is drink coffee all night. My stomach feels horrible."

"Well, let's get some food into you," said Gina, rising and walking to the buffet table. She dished up a full plate of food including a danish and a cinnamon roll, then set it in front of Maggie.

Then she sat down and tucked into her own food again, crunching on the crisp, but meaty bacon. Marsha was eating a cinnamon roll.

Maggie ate some of the eggs and said, "Oh my, this is wonderful. I might have to hire those other two girls permanently. Although I'd look like a blimp in two months time."

"I know what you mean," said Gina. "I dislike cooking so much these days that there's not much tempting to eat around my house."

"Do you live alone?" asked Maggie.

"Just me and the two cats. Although my daughter's come to stay and said she might take me up on my offer to stay for a time. I think she's getting tired of roaming the world. For a few weeks, at least."

Martin came in the room and said, "Good morning all. There's a call for you Maggie, from your brother Ian." He held out a cell phone.

"Oh," said Maggie, wiping her mouth. "Hello Ian."

She listened to someone speaking for a while.

"No, I'm all right. Jennifer and Marsha are here. And Tristan's family are still coming out. I don't know if they'll stay here or on the mainland yet."

During the rest of her short conversation Gina ate and she and Marsha looked at each other.

"I'm worried about her," Marsha mouthed to Gina, when Maggie wasn't looking at them.

Gina nodded in agreement.

"Let's get her outside after breakfast," Gina mouthed back.

Marsha gave her a thumbs up and returned to her cinnamon roll.

"Okay," said Maggie. "Thanks for calling. I'm glad you can cancel your tickets and get the money refunded. And I appreciate your offer. We'll see what the sheriff turns up. It might be natural causes. So we'll just have to see. At any rate, no one's leaving the island. I'll keep in touch. Bye." She clicked the phone off and set it on the table.

"One of my brothers. I talked to his wife last night, he was working."

"In the middle of the night?" asked Marsha.

"He's in Italy, so it wasn't the middle of the night. He's offered to send someone up who he worked with once. A private detective. I hope it doesn't come to that," said Maggie.

"I hope so too," said Marsha.

Maggie just sat there, staring into space.

"Eat," said Gina.

"Oh, I forgot," said Maggie. She picked up her fork and began eating again.

"After breakfast, why don't we take a walk in the garden? You can show me your favorite places and I'll take some photographs and decide what to paint," said Gina. "And after you're good and tired out, you can go back inside and go to bed."

"I could use some fresh air. And a walk," said Maggie. "I need to get my mind off Tristan's relatives."

"Stop worrying about them," said Marsha. "Jennifer and I will take care of them if they show up. We'll stick to you like glue. And if they become rude, you can bet we'll deal with them. We've dealt with plenty of rude people before. And we'll call Martin and Larry if they get really abusive."

"Who's Larry?" asked Gina.

Maggie laughed, "Larry's our mechanic, handyman, fixer of broken things. If something won't work, we call him. He's a genius with all things mechanical. He's also 6'5" and strong.

Gentle as a lamb, but looks a bit scary if you don't know him. Bearded and burly we call him. And Martin's a black belt in something or other. He's always working out in the gym here."

A gym. Of course they had a gym.

Maggie and Gina finished eating and went outside. Marsha went back to her room.

It was eleven and the temperature must be approaching sixty already. It was warm for the end of April, but she wasn't complaining.

They walked through a section filled with *Rhododendron* in their full glory. Reds, pinks, purples and whites dominated one part and as they rounded a bend, yellows and oranges came into view. There were *Crocus*, *Scilla*, and *Narcissus* planted beneath the flowering shrubs. One pale pink rhody, which must be a *Loderi*, sent its sweetness on a breeze that perfumed that part of the garden. The shrub was at least fifteen foot tall and had been limbed up so it formed a tree with many branches.

Gina had seen so many rhody gardens, they weren't uncommon in the northwest, but this one was among the more spectacular. They were interspersed with other flowering shrubs: tree peonies, *Weigela* and *Spirea* so that the color would be carried on once the rhodies were finished blooming.

"Who designed your garden?" Gina asked.

"Oh, our gardener, Dustin, and I did. I buy exotic and exiting plants, and he figures out where to put them. He also buys plants and propagates a great many things. We have a wonderful partnership and he's always open to suggestion. Although he does tell me when something I want to do won't work. I've learned to listen, because he's done the research and he's rarely wrong."

"I hope I get a chance to meet him. Your garden is spectacular. The way things are put together, the flow, the plant choices. You really should let people come and tour it more often."

"All our guests have the time, but not the inclination."

"I meant gardeners. You should offer up your garden for public tours. Charge a fee and donate it to, I don't know. Perhaps the Everett Arboretum. Or one of the Seattle plant groups. This garden deserves to be shared."

"Do you think it's good enough?" asked Maggie.

"I've toured many, many gardens. Yours is right up there with the best."

"Well, that might be something fun to do. We could have Paul ferry people over on the Maggie. I'll look around online and contact some of them. Maybe we can put something together. A fundraiser for them."

"I've gone on a lot of garden tours. The owners always seem to be having a great time networking."

They continued walking through the garden as the sun climbed higher in the sky. Gina loved spring. The hummingbirds were out in full force, clicking warnings at each other and visiting the flowers. Lilac and *Daphne* spread their sweet scents over the entire garden. Plant growth was new and still mostly unmarred by hungry slugs and snails. Peonies were raising their red fingerlike new growth looking like alien creatures rising up from the soil. The air had begun to warm up and hint at the possibility summer might return again. Velvety leaves of lamb's ears were filling out. The garden was a wealth of sensation.

"I think I should go get some sleep," said Maggie. "Thank

you for dragging me out here. The garden really does take my mind off of things. I needed that."

"Nature does that and you're welcome. I think I have enough to photograph right now. I might even pull out a sketchpad later today," said Gina.

THURSDAY AFTERNOON

Gina continued walking around and taking photos with her phone. Her old camera was so outdated, she rarely used it anymore. The phone took better photos and they went directly to her laptop. The changes in technology in her lifetime were truly amazing. Difficult to navigate at first, but she was slowly learning.

She came upon a section of the garden filled with a dozen small flowering trees. Apples? Maybe cherries or plums? She couldn't remember how to tell one type of fruit tree from another unless they had fruit on them. The flowers' sweet scent smelled wonderful and the air filled with the sound of buzzing bees. Bumblebees and orchard mason bees. They were happily pollinating the white and pink flowered trees. The ground surrounding the trees was covered with sprawling hardy geraniums. In no time they'd open their pink or purple flowers about the size of a nickel.

Following the path around a bend, she discovered a small

patio with a white cast iron table and chairs. Emma sat at the table.

Doing nothing. No phone. Not crying. Just staring into space. Then Gina saw that this section was outside one of the bedrooms, the glass door wide open.

"Oh, excuse me. I didn't mean to intrude. I didn't realize anyone was out in the garden."

"No problem," said Emma.

"Are you okay?" asked Gina.

"I don't know. I feel sort of numb."

"Well, that's certainly understandable."

"I should be crying. Tearing my hair out."

"You know, there's no right way to grieve," said Gina.

"But even my mom's crying and upset. So is the maid. Why can't I cry?" wailed Emma.

Gina pulled out a chair and sat down.

"Because you're different. You have different feelings."

"I'm so mad. Why did he have to die? And I was so mad at him all day yesterday."

"Why?"

"Stupid stuff. He told me he was having an affair. Three damn days before the wedding. But he still wanted to get married. He just wasn't going to give her up. Told me he couldn't be a one-woman man."

"Well, if I were you, I'd be mad too. Doesn't mean you didn't love him. My late husband and I fought. We got mad at each other. But love does tend to heal things in the end."

"I didn't kill him, but I wanted to. Did you ever feel that way?"

"Frequently," said Gina. "I remember one time, we were short on money. And he had a bit too much to drink at an office party and totaled the car. He walked away unscathed, luckily. I was so angry. We had to come up with enough money to buy a new car, because the insurance money wasn't enough. Our rates went up. Then there was the ticket. I wanted to strangle him. Plus we had three toddlers and no car for a couple of weeks. At Christmas!"

Emma laughed.

"I remember trying to get all three girls on the bus to go downtown and shop for Christmas gifts for my relatives, he wasn't getting one that year. Shopping like that was something I never repeated again."

"But it all came right in the end. With Tristan it never will," Emma said. Her face wrinkled up and she began to weep.

Gina scooched her chair over and put an arm around Emma's shoulders.

"There were so many good things about him. And so many bad ones too," said Emma

"He was human then. What things didn't you like about him?"

"He was an arrogant ass so much of the time. Going on about Uncle Ian's fat belly. Made me so mad. Then again, he's never seen Uncle Ian. I told him about all my relatives in confidence."

"And he betrayed that."

"Yes. And betrayed me. Having another lover. I thought I was the only one. Silly me. I mean, I didn't think I would always be the only one. But I thought he might wait a few years, maybe months, after the wedding. And his bad business deals, ..."

Gina interrupted her, "How were they bad?"

"He owed money everywhere. And cheated people. He wasn't ethical, not like Dad."

"What kind of business was he in?"

"Import-export. All sorts of things, some of them really dodgy."

"He must have had some good qualities. Reasons you fell in love with him."

"He was charming. Handsome. A great dancer and fun to talk to. But all of that's so superficial. Mom and Dad taught me better. I guess I felt so happy that such a wonderful man fell for me. He always treated me so well. Until he told me there was someone else." Emma paused, then said, "I guess it was all fake."

"He did say he loved you. Wanted to marry you. Perhaps that was real."

"Perhaps," said Emma, wiping tears away. "But it wasn't enough. Was it?"

"Not for many of us. If you need someone who will love only you, then no. I wouldn't have wanted to share my husband."

"Did your husband ever? ..."

"No, I think three daughters kept him far too busy. And I kept him busy too. Our lives were always so complicated. Then when he retired, we moved to the country and he died."

"I'm sorry," said Emma.

"Well, we all die. Nothing can change that," said Gina, looking at her wrinkled hands sitting on the table.

"Thank you for stopping to talk to me. Why is it easier to talk to you than Mom or Aunt Jenny?" She wiped her face again and straightened her black t-shirt.

"Because I'm a complete stranger," said Gina.

"It should be harder."

"No, I don't have an agenda for you. And I have grown three daughters."

"So what would you advise your daughter to do in my place?"

"I'd advise her to cry if she needed to. To find a soundproof place to yell if she needed to. To find a punching bag if that would help. To let it all out. To talk to someone if that helped. But the important thing is to grieve in her own way and then to heal. To come back to life and grow again. And realize that grieving takes time. To be patient and love herself. I know it sounds like a cliche, but it's true."

"Thank you. I will think about that. Everything seems so muddled right now."

"Because you're walking around in the fog. It's always that way when we're in the middle of things. The fog will clear," said Gina.

"Okay. Maybe I should go sleep."

"Did you sleep at all last night?"

"No. I paced around my rooms and the garden. Cursing him under my breath, and feeling guilty about it."

"Go inside, have Martin bring you a cup of warm milk, drink it and sleep as long as you need to."

"Thank you, I think I will. A cup of warm milk sounds good right now."

Emma got up from her chair and walked away.

Then she turned back and said, "Thank you, again. I hope I'm as wise when I get to be your age."

Emma walked through the bedroom door and out of sight.

Gina leaned back in the chair. She didn't feel wise.

She also didn't know if Emma was an extraordinary actress and had actually poisoned her fiancé or if she was innocent.

Gina sighed and glanced at her watch. It was nearly one. Her stomach rumbled. What time was lunch around here? Perhaps she should go in and find out. Figure out who else she could pump for information.

Paul? Maybe Martin. She didn't think she'd have much luck with Martin. He didn't seem to miss much, but she had a feeling he was intensely loyal. And it wouldn't be to Tristan. She wouldn't have much of a chance of getting anything out of Martin. No, she'd leave him to the sheriff.

The other staff, maybe. She could go hang out in the kitchen. Chat with the cook. Or cooks. Maybe they heard or saw something that would give her a clue.

The dining room was empty. So she wandered through the swinging wooden door that the cooks had come through last night.

The industrial kitchen was a large room. Painted a warm peach color which made the room feel warmer in contrast to all the stainless steel that defined it as a commercial-sized kitchen. It held large mixers and an entire corner with a dishwasher like Gina had seen only in restaurants. A wall full of stacked ovens and an eight burner heavy duty gas stove. The wooden island was at least ten feet long and six feet wide. Covered with vegetables ready to be chopped: carrots, potatoes and onions.

Two women stood at an open oven, consulting over a sheet of cookies. Another came out of a large door that brought a rush of cold air into the warm room. A walk-in cooler. Or freezer. Or both.

"Hello," said Gina.

The woman who'd come out of the walk-in brushed a strand of her light brown hair with blond highlights back, tucking it into the long braid the hair had escaped from, and said, "Hello. What can I help you with?"

"I don't know when lunch is served," said Gina.

"Normally, at noon, but it seems everyone's on different schedules today. So, lunch is served whenever you want it."

She had regal features and looked strong and wiry. One of those women who would look at home on a hiking trail or the dance floor.

"If it's not an interruption I'd like to eat soon."

"What would you like?"

"I'm up for almost anything," said Gina.

"Sandwich?"

"Perfect."

In the end Gina had a roast beef sandwich with horseradish and arugula. She chose to sit in the kitchen at a small wooden table, rather than the formal dining room all alone.

"Thank you for being so agreeable. I'm Tiffany."

"Gina."

"You're the artist. I love your paintings."

"Thank you."

"This is Katie," she pointed to a slender woman with purple hair who waved. Her hands full of a loaded pastry bag.

"And Julie." Julie was a tall, blonde Amazon emptying a fifty pound bag of flour into a large plastic bin. Without filling the kitchen with a cloud of flour. Julie nodded a hello in their direction.

"Where did all of you meet?"

"We used to work at the same bakery, at a grocery store. It

was an awful place to work. Everything was made from mixes. We eventually all left to work in restaurants, but stayed in touch over the years. And we call each other when there's a good job opening. Like for this wedding," said Tiffany.

"And now you're all stuck here, trying to deal with way too much food for far too few people," said Gina.

"Well, it's a challenge. We'll be canning and freezing some of the fruit and veggies. But yes, we've had to reinvent the menu for the next few days. But we're having fun and we're together. But you're stuck here too."

"And I can tell you, it's such a hardship to be stuck out in that horrible, horrible garden." Gina laughed and the others joined her.

"It's true, this is the best job I've ever had," said Tiffany. "It's tough to get supplies on a moment's notice, but Maggie is willing to spend extra to keep everything stocked up. She's a very generous employer. And the island is beautiful. Plus, there's the exquisite kitchen garden out that door to harvest yummy things from."

"I haven't seen the kitchen garden yet. What fun! And you live here, year round?"

"Yes, it does limit the people I get to see. Then again, I've always valued my solitude."

"There's a few more people here now than there usually is, am I right?"

"Well Jennifer and Marsha come out often. And Emma. Tristan did. But Maggie and Paul entertain a lot. Often guests come and stay for weeks, sometimes months."

"Did Tristan and Emma get along well?" asked Gina, hoping she hadn't stepped over a line. And that they'd answer her question. "It's such a sad thing."

"Funny you should mention that," said Tiffany, glancing at Katie.

"Why?"

"Katie overheard them arguing yesterday."

"Really, what did you hear?"

Katie looked at Tiffany. Tiffany nodded as if to say it didn't matter now.

Katie said, "I went out to the gym to collect dirty dishes. Martin works out everyday, so do some of the other staff and there's always dishes left lying around. Emma and Tristan were in the gym, pretending to play tennis. They were standing with the net between them, screaming at each other at the top of their lungs. The most horrid things. She called him a cheating bastard. He called her a stuck up, well, I won't even say the word. Gutter talk. It continued on the entire time I was in the foyer, collecting dirty glasses. They must have been able to see I was there—the partition is made of clear glass—but they didn't stop. Just kept on going, yelling. She got mad and threw her racket on the gym floor. I could hear it break. And she stomped out, right past me. He went out the other door, slamming it."

"Did you tell the Sheriff?" asked Gina.

"I haven't had a chance to talk to him yet," said Katie. "Should I? It would make Emma look really bad. She couldn't have murdered him, could she?"

Katie was obviously very naive.

"If she murdered Tristan doesn't she deserve to pay for that?" asked Gina.

"Yes, you're right," said Katie.

Gina said, "The Sheriff is a good man. If we tell him everything we know, it will help him find out the truth.

Anything that's suspicious or out of the ordinary. He needs to know everything."

"You know him?" asked Tiffany.

"I was painting at a nursery last year when the owners were murdered. He managed to find and catch the murderers even though the circumstances were really challenging."

"Challenging in what way?" asked Julie, joining in the conversation.

"There was a plant conference in the area and the attendees were touring the gardens. There were hundreds of people, any one of whom could have murdered the owners. It was a challenge for him to sift through all of them."

"Wow," said Julie. "And that's why I'm a baker!"

They laughed.

Gina finished her lunch, refusing the third cookie they tried to press on her.

"It's my grandma's recipe," said Katie.

"I just can't. I'm stuffed. I'm sure someone needs it though."

Gina left the kitchen, thinking about what Katie had said. Emma had told her about some of the argument, but perhaps not the violence of it. Slamming her tennis racket to the floor so hard she broke it. Did she do that sort of thing a lot? Another question to ask.

Still, often people with explosive tempers got their blowups out of the way and then returned to normal as if nothing had happened. Was Emma one of those people? Or had it made her want to kill Tristan?

There was a message on her phone when she checked. She'd turned the ringer to silent. Sheriff Jansson said he was coming out around three and he had some questions for her. She glanced at the time. It was one.

"I guess that is unusual," Maggie paused. "Oh hello darling. Aren't you making a run to pick people up?"

"No. The sheriff's bringing them over. Probably on his way right now, I understand. Maybe we can get this all over with soon."

Gina took a deep breath. That was interesting. Why had Maggie needed to change the subject when Paul was near? Didn't want to be seen gossiping with the help? The man must be the gardener, otherwise why would they have been talking about the shrub?

Or had there been another reason Maggie didn't want to talk about the murder near Paul? Was she having an affair with the gardener and discussing the murder would show a closeness that shouldn't be there?

Or did Maggie suspect Paul?

Gina kept working, layering in more detail on the painting, while continuing to mull over the possibilities.

Maggie and Paul's voices came closer, moving around the end of the hedge. They must have left the gardener behind. Gina could smell Maggie's strong orange and musk perfume before she realized they were so close.

"Oh, hello Gina. I didn't know you were out here painting. You're so quiet," said Paul.

"I've been concentrating. Trying to capture the music of this bed."

"It's so beautiful," said Maggie, with a hint of tightness in her voice.

"Thank you," said Gina. "When I paint a scene this complex I get so caught up in my own little bubble that I have no idea what's going on in the world."

"Oh, you're in a flow state, then," said Maggie.

Her voice sounded relieved.

"I guess I am. I forget to eat, don't pay attention to the time."

"Did you get lunch?" asked Paul.

"I did. I had a wonderful sandwich and chatted with the ladies in the kitchen. It was great."

"I eat in the kitchen a lot," said Paul. "But Tiffany's usually in there with no one to keep her company. She's really having fun with her friends here."

Gina put her brush in the jar of water and rinsed it out. Adding anything else to the painting would just ruin it. For her, the most important piece of making art was knowing when to stop.

"Oh, are you done?" asked Maggie.

"I am," said Gina.

"I think we should plan on buying everything you paint while you're here," said Paul. "If you're willing to sell your paintings, that is."

"I hadn't given it any thought. Why would you want to buy things sight unseen?" asked Gina.

"Well, I seem to love everything you paint," said Paul. "And it seems only right since you're trapped here."

"Was it your fault that I'm trapped here?" asked Gina.

"Well, no, ..."

"Then I think you should ignore that reason. I'll take a look at the paintings when I'm done and see if I think they're salable. If they are, I'll give you the first chance to buy them," Gina said.

His offer made her feel uneasy, like he was pushing her. Gina didn't like to be manipulated and certainly wasn't going to be pushed into selling something she thought was substandard. And she certainly didn't want charity purchases.

"That sounds fair," said Paul.

"Deal, then," said Maggie. "I really do love this painting though. This is one of my favorite spots in the garden at this time of year. And it's so fleeting. The *Arisaema* and trout lilies fade as summer begins and the *Hosta* overwhelm everything. I love summer too, but spring is so special here. There's a delicacy about all the plants."

"Oh, I so agree," said Gina. "This section is just lovely. Mind you, I haven't seen the entire garden yet, but the blooms in this bed are so fleeting, I just had to paint them first."

Martin came from the direction of the house and said, "The sheriff is here. Along with Mr. and Mrs. Matthews."

Maggie's face drooped and she looked about ten years older in just one moment. Gina wanted to reach out and hug her. The woman looked devastated.

Paul turned to Gina. "Tristan's parents."

Then he asked, "Where are they, Martin?"

"They're all in the parlor. Or rather that's where I left them. The sheriff tends to wander."

"Well, it's his job, let him wander. We've got nothing to hide. We'll be right in. Oh, make sure they have some refreshments."

"Already done," Martin said, pivoted on one foot and returned to the house.

"Well, we better get this done," said Paul.

"It's not going to get any easier, is it?" said Maggie. She took a deep breath and Gina watched as the woman forced her face into a mask of calm compassion and took Paul's arm. They followed the path Martin had taken back to the house.

Gina was half torn. She wanted to be a fly on the wall during that conversation. Then again, she wouldn't learn anything. Maggie and Paul were both putting their best foot forward. Their masks wouldn't slip. And she didn't really want to be part of the Matthews' grief or anger.

She was done painting this section of the garden and it had moved into deep shade and felt chilly now. She dumped her paint water onto the soil. Then packed everything up and returned to her room, where she washed her brushes and the water container. Leaving them perched near the bathroom sink to dry.

She washed her hands with the minty soap, then ran her damp hands over her hair, trying to get it back into place. Checked her clothes for paint stains and found none, although she'd worn the busy floral print shirt for just that reason. It rarely showed stains or spills.

Afterwards, Gina walked through the house to search for the sheriff.

She didn't find him in Tristan's room, which still had crime scene tape over the closed door, and after knocking continued walking down all the hallways. She finally ended with the main common rooms.

Moving quickly past the open parlor door, she heard Paul, Maggie and two other voices whom she assumed were Tristan's parents. They were having a heated discussion.

She found the sheriff in the warm kitchen talking to the cooks. The kitchen smelled divine. Basil, onions and tomatoes were the predominant scents, which made her mouth water. She hoped that was dinner cooking.

"Oh hello," Gina said.

Sheriff Jansson washed down a bite of cookie with some

coffee. "Gina, good to see you. I was going to come looking for you after I finished here."

"Should I come back later?" she asked, raising her eyebrow at the plate of cookies.

"No, you're welcome to stay. Katie said you were the one who suggested that she talk to me."

"Yes," said Gina.

Tiffany held out the serving plate full of cookies to Gina.

"No thanks," she said.

Then realized she was hungry. "Okay, maybe just one."

Gina took a chocolate chip cookie and bit into it. Buttery, chocolate flavor filled her mouth. "This is wonderful."

"Thank you," said Tiffany. "Help yourself to some coffee."

Gina poured herself a cup after realizing how tired she felt. She probably wasn't going to get that nap this afternoon.

Then sat at the kitchen table while listening to Katie's story again. The sheriff took notes and listened intently.

After Katie finished, he asked, "I'm going to have to ask you, did you know Tristan before you came here to the island?"

"No, not at all," said Katie.

"What about you Julie?"

"Never set eyes on him."

"But you knew him some, right Tiffany? He'd been here before this trip."

"Yes. I knew him from when I served meals. He never came into the kitchen. I never actually talked to him, which was fine with me."

"Why?"

"Well, he was sort of a jerk."

"How?"

"He was always making snotty jokes. You know the kind that are partly true? Teasing Maggie about her weight. Emma about her long nose. Telling Paul he was old, Martin that he had a stick up his butt. I don't like that sort of humor, making fun of people when there's not much they can do to change things. Especially when it's about my friends. But I didn't kill him. Emma would have dumped him sooner or later, after she figured out who he really was. She's a smart woman."

"So you think he was worse than he let on around her?" asked the sheriff.

"Yes I do. I don't have any real reason for thinking that. But I'm a good judge of people and he wasn't a nice man. He treated all the *hired help* like dirt. People who do that are the real scum of the earth. It just takes time for everyone else to see that."

"Did any of the other employees know Tristan?"

"Not that they mentioned to me. Although I don't talk much to Tom. He mostly stays on the Maggie," said Tiffany.

"But Gayle, ..." said Julie.

"What about Gayle?" asked the sheriff.

"Gayle was going on about Tristan. Mooning about his blond hair and those big blue eyes," said Julie, snorting. "As if he were God's gift to women. I don't think she knew him, not enough to see the real person. She saw him as a lust item."

The sheriff looked at Tiffany.

"It's true," she said. "Gayle's young, just eighteen. She hasn't been out in the world much yet. Saving money for college or until she figures out what to do with her life. She's sort of at loose ends—emotionally. And there aren't any young single men on the island. So she did go on a lot about Tristan. Not around Emma or Maggie, you understand. But in the

74

kitchen when just us women were around. She didn't know him but was always going out of her way to do little things to make his room perfect. The extra mile, you know?"

"Tell me," said the sheriff.

"Oh bringing him an extra towel before he asked for it. Making sure he had fresh flowers in his room every day. That sort of thing."

"Does the housekeeper, Sheila, do that sort of thing?" asked the sheriff.

"Extra towels? Not unless someone asks for it. I think flowers are changed out on a weekly basis or freshened if they need it. Not every day. Sheila's more level-headed. Then again she's much older. Gayle's still a silly young girl, which is cute, but a bit wearing." Tiffany smiled.

"Okay, well I'm sure I'll have more questions. If any of you have anything to add, anything at all—no matter how tiny the detail—feel free to call me. Leave a message if I don't pick up, okay? Sometimes it's the tiniest detail that solves the case for me. You have my card?"

They nodded their heads.

"All right then, thanks for the cookies and coffee. I might just have to move in here."

The cooks all laughed at his joke.

He smiled and got up from the table. Gina drained her cup of strong coffee, set the cup in a plastic bin of dirty dishes, then grabbed another cookie to go. She followed him outside through the kitchen door.

There were two patio tables with chairs out on the area paved with old red brick. One with an umbrella which made shade beneath it and another sitting in the still-bright sun. The garden here was a beautifully laid out kitchen garden.

Most of the beds were still bare, waiting warmer temperatures. The ones in use contained mustard greens, rainbow chard and at least six different types of lettuce. There were onions, or maybe they were garlic. And trellises of snow peas and sugar snap peas. Carrot and radish tops poked up through the dark rich soil. A huge bed of asparagus stood nearby, almost ready to pick.

There were also beds of blooming strawberry plants, rows of heavily pruned raspberries and other berries she didn't know. At least two beds were full of herbs. Gina spotted oregano, bronze fennel and thyme, as well as several other herbs she couldn't identify by sight. Six dwarf fruit trees were placed throughout the garden, in a lovely pattern.

"Sun or shade?" the sheriff asked.

"Sun, definitely sun. I'm still starved for it after such a rainy winter."

They sat at the small table and the sun warmed her skin. She'd taken her sweater off and wrapped it around her waist, while washing up the painting supplies.

"Well, the coroner gave me a provisional heads-up that Tristan was poisoned. She wasn't entirely sure what was used. That will have to wait for the autopsy, but she indicated it was possibly Aconite poisoning. The plant is common enough, but the use of it as an effective poison is relatively rare. One of the first signs to appear is profuse vomiting, which you might have noticed in Tristan's room. She said the whole plant is toxic, roots, leaves, seeds. Have you seen any of that growing around here?"

"Aconite." She tried to place the plant name, wishing she'd spent more time studying names. "Aconite, is that monkshood?"

He looked in his notebook, "Yes, that was the other name she used."

"I don't know. I don't recall it, but I haven't been through all the gardens yet and I wasn't looking for it, so I could easily have missed it or forgotten. There are so many different plants here. And even if it was growing in the garden, it might be in the compost pile or tossed out into the woods by now."

"Yes, you're right of course," he said.

"Was it in the wine?"

"Most likely. The test results aren't back yet, but she said wine might have been used to cover the taste. Especially a strong wine like port."

"Do you have anyone you think had a reason to kill him?" Gina asked.

"I've got at least a dozen people. Some of them are even on this island."

"Who?"

"Paul, Maggie, Emma to name just a few," he said.

Gina had no answer for that.

"I don't have any way to eliminate most of the people on this island from the equation. Some are less likely than others to have wanted him dead."

"Who are closest to elimination?" asked Gina.

"Well you, all the cooks and Sheila, the housekeeper. Larry the mechanic/handyman. Marsha and Jennifer seem rather unlikely at this point as well."

"And you're sure Tristan was the intended recipient of the poison?" Gina asked.

"No. Right now I'm sure of very little."

"Does Paul know he might be the one who was supposed to be murdered?"

"I dropped that on him early this morning before I left. He was suitably disturbed by the thought."

"And did that tell you anything?"

"No. He's a man in control of everything around him. He lives on an island and controls who comes and goes. He's charming, and at first glance, easy going. But don't let that fool you. He's in complete charge of everything here. And I don't think much escapes him."

Gina said, "So, the entire house and gardens could be under surveillance then, right?"

"Possibly. I asked if there were cameras and Paul said no. I would think someone who was observant would have noticed cameras out in the garden, such as the gardener. Then again hidden cameras have become an art form and even if surveillance was just picking up sound, it's easy to hide. I know I wouldn't have an art collection like he does, displayed out in the open, without having a lot of security. I've seen no muscle around."

"Martin?"

"Possibly. A good bodyguard doesn't necessarily need to look like one."

"Certainly not Larry?"

"The mechanic/handyman? No, he's a gentle soul. I think he'd be helpful in a pinch, but he's not a trained fighter. He's just big."

"Interesting," said Gina. All of this was out of her realm of experience.

"Yes."

"So how long are you going to keep everyone here?" asked Gina.

"Longing for home?"

"No, not really. But I don't want to be the next victim either."

"I need to keep this locked down for a bit longer. I've let Tristan's parents come. They needed to talk to Paul and Maggie, it's the least I could do seeing as how they can't get his body back for several days. I'll take them back with me tonight, unless they decide to stay. I'm leaving Deputy Hofsteader here till tomorrow. Just in case."

"In case of what?"

"In case they decide to murder Paul in his bed? In case gossip breaks loose."

"What sort of gossip?"

"Anything that's helpful."

"So, there's nothing more I need to listen out for?" asked Gina.

"No. Please keep your ears open. And your eyes. See if you can locate that plant, but don't touch it. I want to see if it's been recently cut."

"I can do that."

"And I need to talk to that gardener. After you find the plant."

"So I shouldn't ask him about it?"

The sheriff gave her a baleful look.

"Okay, not a good joke," she said.

"It was beneath you."

"What are you going to do next?" she asked.

"I'm still interviewing staff."

"What's the deputy doing?"

"Collecting more evidence."

"You didn't finish last night?"

"You mean this morning. No. We found a few other things to look for."

He obviously wasn't going to tell her, so she didn't even ask. The warm sun was making her sleepy. Gina didn't know if she could stay awake through dinner. She'd certainly make it an early night tonight.

The sheriff said, "Well, I'd better get on with things."

"Okay, I'll see you later," she said, leaning back against the chair and closing her eyes.

"Don't fall asleep. Someone might take the rest of that cookie," he said, pointing at her half eaten cookie.

"Then I guess I'll still be hungry for dinner."

"If you insist," he said, snatching the cookie and walking back into the kitchen.

She laughed. She really hadn't needed the second cookie.

THURSDAY EVENING

Gina did fall asleep, only to be woken by the dinner gong.

She sat up and realized it had grown cold outside. The entire patio had long been in the shade. She rubbed her hands over her face and stood up.

Going back in through the kitchen door, she walked through the kitchen. All three women bustled about, two filling serving bowls and the other sautéeing up something that smelled delicious.

Gina went down the hallway to the dining room. Maggie, Paul, Jennifer and Marsha were there. As well as two strangers who had to be the Matthews. Emma hadn't arrived yet.

The long table had been divided into three smaller ones, two of which were pushed against a wall and decorated with flowers. The remaining table seated everyone comfortably with a few spare places to add more people in.

She sat down next to Marsha and across from Jennifer and as far away from the Matthews as possible. The room was absolutely silent. Gina put her napkin in her lap and sipped water from her glass. Her mouth had felt dry and the water tasted refreshing.

It seemed a very long time till Emma came in. Her eyes were red and puffy with circles beneath them. She'd obviously spent the last several hours crying.

Emma went over to Mrs. Matthews and hugged her. The older woman stiffened, then seemed to relax into the hug. Emma held her hand out to Mr. Matthews. He took her hand and held it for a time.

Emma said, "I'm glad the two of you came out. I wish, ..."

"I know dear," said Mr. Matthews, patting Emma's hand.

Emma took a seat near Mrs. Matthews.

Both the Matthews were very dressed up. He wore a dark blue business suit and tie. She wore a navy skirt, white blouse, stockings and heels, and a modest amount of gold jewelry. Both of them were slender and Gina guessed, in their early forties. They looked rather elegant in a conservative way. Both of them also looked completely overdressed for dinner. Perhaps they were making a statement or perhaps that was how they always dressed.

They weren't wearing black though, which conservative people usually did after a death in the family. That puzzled Gina.

"Now that everyone's here, I'll make introductions while the appetizers are brought in," said Paul. He stood up and walked behind Mr. Matthews.

"This is Sam Matthews, Tristan's father."

Paul continued moving around the table, as he said everyone's names.

"And Maggie, or Margaret, but don't call her that or she'll spit at you." Maggie slapped at his hand in jest.

"And her sister, Jennifer Donahue. And our visiting painter, Gina Wetherby. And Jennifer's partner, Marsha Ritter. And our lovely Emma. Last, but certainly not least, Natalie Matthews, Tristan's mother."

Then Paul circled back to his own chair and signaled to Martin who'd been almost invisibly standing near the open kitchen door. Martin went into the kitchen and returned with two plates, followed by the cooks, carrying several plates each.

The appetizers were mussels cooked with garlic, herbs and butter, with little toasts to spread them on. What were the toasts called? Crostini? She couldn't remember.

Gina ate hers, although she wasn't a shellfish fan. They were almost palatable.

Just as she cleared her plate, Martin swooped it away and was gone. When everyone had finished, out came the green salads.

The salad was just as good as the one from the previous night. Young spring greens, sharp and bitter, mixed with delicate lettuces. A balsamic vinegar and oil dressing with lots of fresh garlic and sprinkled with soft goat cheese.

Gina noticed soft classical music playing over the sound system. It hadn't been there last night. But last night the conversation was lively and jovial, full of hope for the coming wedding. Tonight the only people talking were Jennifer and Marsha.

"So we tried to dive today. I can't remember the last time I even swam. I was going for the most basic of basic dives. Managed a belly flop and didn't kill myself. I'm calling it a win," said Jennifer

Maggie gave a weak smile.

Marsha said, "You should have seen her, she could barely breathe for ten minutes. I nearly called Martin to give her CPR."

Both she and Jennifer laughed. Gina saw Natalie crack a smile, then replace it with a sad look.

The rest of the dinner went the same way. It was difficult to inject any levity because really, Tristan's parents were mourning their son. And Emma, her fiancé. Paul and Maggie may or may not have been in mourning over Tristan's death, but they had to be in shock. They'd been planning the wedding for months, maybe years, and now the ground had shifted out from beneath their feet.

The only good thing was the food. The lasagne Gina had smelled cooking earlier was the best she'd ever tasted. Dessert was a choice of vanilla, chocolate or lavender ice cream. Gina had a scoop of each one, but found herself most fond of the lavender. It tasted like summer on a spoon. All the ice creams had been made in the kitchen. Those cooks were amazing. She had to get off the island soon or her clothes wouldn't fit any more.

There was coffee after dinner, Gina opted for mint tea. No one drank any port. Then as soon as politely possible, she excused herself for a walk in the garden.

"I really need to get some exercise," she said. "I've done nothing but eat since I got here. And I still haven't seen the entire garden yet."

"Oh, how I wish I could go with you," Maggie whispered to her. "But alas, I'm doing penance."

"For what?"

"Being the hostess and having a murder occur under my roof."

Maggie's back was to the room, and to the Matthews. Otherwise, Gina felt sure she never would have said such a thing.

"I'll be fine on my own. Clears my head."

She left the room. What a sad life these people must have. Even without a murder. To feel so responsible for one's guests. Yet, she would probably feel the same if a guest had died at her house. There certainly wouldn't be as many suspects at her place. Herself and the cats. That was it. The cats would likely kill anyone who got between them and their food. Case solved.

Gina went out the main entry and into the gardens on the left. She hadn't been on this side of the house. It was full of Japanese Maples just leafing out. Their spring colors of pink, red, orange and lime green were spectacular. Someone, the gardener she assumed, knew how to prune. Each tree or small shrub was absolutely perfect. In amongst the maples were shore pines, also elaborately pruned.

Tidy *Rhododendron* plants, some in bloom, were sprinkled throughout the beds. Some of the beds were covered with well-behaved ground covers. Others were populated with ferns, *Epimedium*, with their delicate, starry flowers and more pink, cream and yellow trout and fawn lilies. It wasn't strictly a Japanese garden, more a Pacific Northwest garden in the Japanese style. Not a leaf out of place. There were mounds of bamboo with beautifully striped culms. Then down a walkway and on each side of the pristine gravel path, forests of giant timber bamboo.

Gina forgot about looking for the *Aconitum*. She felt so entranced with the quiet solitude of this lovely garden. The tall timber bamboo forest was majestic. It looked like it had been there for decades and as if it went on for miles on either side of the path. She wouldn't have been able to wrap one hand around some of the stalks and have her fingers meet.

She followed the walkway as it curved and opened out onto a splash of color. Peonies surrounded her, their fluffy-floofy blossoms scented the air with sweetness. Poking out from between them were bearded iris in exotic colors. There were roses there, not yet in bud. And a *Weigela* or two, flower buds still tight and not ready to open yet. Tall lilacs, in full bloom, bordered the back of the bed.

She'd have to come back and photograph the bearded iris. She'd left her phone in her room. But the light was waning anyway.

Then around the next bend was a part shade bed. Filled with deep blue, white, and bicolor *Aconitum*. Masses of them. Tall stalks of hooded flowers waving in the breeze, looking not at all threatening. If there ever was a flower which looked as if it should house a fairy, this was it.

She looked to see if some had been cut, but the mass of them prevented her from seeing far into the bed. She'd leave that to the sheriff.

Why hadn't she brought her phone? She could call Sheriff Jansson right now. Silly, silly, silly. Well, at least she knew where this bed was. She could retrace her steps from the front door and find it again.

She kept going forward, trying to find where the path tied into part of the garden she'd been before. Did the garden have a pattern? Was there a map? The house had been laid out in such a specific shape. Surely, the garden was the same. She should ask Maggie. And try to meet the mysterious gardener.

She didn't even know his name.

The path continued on to a woodland garden. Which held several of those very fancy big-leafed rhodies from Asia. Some of them were in bloom, with pristine white flowers, others with pink blossoms so pale they were nearly white. There were also Tasmanian tree ferns. Did the island have that warm of a microclimate? Or did they dig them up every winter and haul them into the greenhouse?

She moved into the next garden which was filled with *Hydrangea* bushes, not yet budded up. Newly planted hardy *Fuchsia*, clearly fresh from the greenhouse, sat at their feet. Gina's hardy *Fuchsia* at home had barely leafed out. These had flower buds on them. The gardener must not be expecting any more frosts. Or perhaps, he'd pulled out all the stops simply for the wedding. The last frost date around here was late May. Although, with the changing climate, the last few springs had gone awry. Sometimes, summer came a month early. Sometimes, it was horribly cold and rainy well into summer.

Gina stopped at a bench in the fading sun and sat down. A long-haired gray tabby cat came out of the garden and meowed at her.

"Well, hello" she said, bending over and holding her hand out and making the ticking sound she used to call her cats.

The cat must have decided she was friendly and came over to get its head scratched and rub against her legs. Its fur felt silky-smooth.

"You're a friendly beast, aren't you? Would you like to come up on my lap?"

She picked the cat up and it happily lay down on her lap, purring and purring.

"Oh, what a sweetie you are."

She found a collar and a tag on it read, Maybelle."

"Maybelle. What a lovely name. Is this your garden?"

Maybelle meowed as to how it was.

"I don't suppose you know who poisoned Tristan, do you? You probably didn't like him. I'm sure he wasn't a cat person. But if you could help me, that would be lovely."

Just then Maybelle's ears perked up and she shot off Gina's lap, giving chase to a squirrel amongst the rhodies.

"Ah well, you've got work to do. Don't let those squirrels eat all the rhody buds. They're quite fond of them, I've heard."

Maybelle vanished from sight into the bushes.

Gina got up and kept walking, finally finding the path that led back to her room. She picked up her phone and called the sheriff. He didn't answer so she left a message. Then saw there was a message from Shelly.

"Hi Mom, just wanted to let you know the cats are still fine. I'm fine. I just can't find your coffeemaker. Or espresso machine. Do you have one? All I can find is tea. Is that all you drink in the morning? Guess I'll take your car down to town and buy one. If you get this, then let me know."

Gina looked at the time of the message. It had been around three. Shelly must be really turned around time-wise if she'd been looking for coffee at three in the afternoon. All that traveling.

She called Shelly who answered after one ring.

"Hi Mom."

"Hello dear. How are you?"

"Fine. A bit tired, but the trip back to the states was very long."

"I'm sorry I didn't get your call. You must have called when

I left my phone in my room. And I forgot to check my messages. Did you get a coffeemaker?"

"I found an awesome one at one of the stores downtown. You didn't already have one, did you?"

"No. I don't normally drink coffee. I quit years ago, when I retired. Switched over to tea."

"Well, that explains all the tea then."

"What are you up to today?"

"I got some food. Mostly I decided to just nap and hang out with your two furballs."

"They'll appreciate that."

"Has the sheriff found out what happened yet?"

"It looks like Tristan has been poisoned, but I don't think the sheriff knows who did it yet."

"Are you sure it's safe for you to be there?"

"Probably. This type of murder is targeted, I think. These people are mostly strangers to me. I'm guessing his death had to do with someone having a bone to pick with him. I just don't know which bone it was."

"Well, stay safe. Don't eat anything strange, just in case."

"Well, at least the food is fantastic. There are three young women in the kitchen, two of whom came over to help out with the wedding food. I'm going to need to buy new clothes if I stay much longer."

Shelly laughed. "You can have mine. I've lost about twenty pounds hiking around in the last three months. I actually had to buy a belt to keep my pants up. I mean to remedy that though. I bought a chocolate cake from the grocery store."

"Did you go to Corr's Grocery?"

"Yeah. I didn't want to go any farther, not off the island. I'm too tired."

"Their cakes are amazing."

"Yes, I know. I've eaten a couple pieces already."

"Well, eat some real food too. I stocked up for you."

"I saw your note, thanks. I will. But life is short, eat dessert first, right?"

"Yes. Oh, I did have the most wonderful chocolate chip cookie today. And homemade ice cream. Oh my goodness."

There was a knock at Gina's door. She opened it and saw Sheriff Jansson standing there. Gina motioned him into the room.

"The sheriff is here. I'll give you a call tomorrow. See if you're less groggy. Eat some vitamins to you make sure you're getting what you need. I don't want you to get sick."

"Okay Mom. Stop worrying and have some fun. Is the sheriff a hottie?"

"I'm not going to dignify that with an answer," said Gina. "Bye."

Her face felt warm and she knew it had turned red. When was the last time that had happened? She couldn't remember.

Gina turned to the sheriff.

"Hello. That was one of my daughters."

"How is she?"

"Jetlagged."

"You sent me a message?" he asked.

"Oh yes. I found the monkshood. A huge bed of it. I'm not sure if that's where it came from or not."

He glanced out the window.

"It's getting a bit dark out," he said. "But if you lead me to it, I can look at it more closely once the sun's up tomorrow morning. When you, like all normal people, will still be sleeping."

"Sure," Gina said.

She grabbed her sweater and pulled it on, sliding the phone into her pant's pocket. She might need the flashlight on it. "We'll need to go out the front door. That's the most direct route, I think. I still haven't figured out the structure of this garden. The paths seem to form a maze from what I can tell."

"Well if you can't figure it out, I'm sure there's no hope for me," he said.

She showed him how to find the monkshood by walking past the Japanese Gardens and through the bamboo forest. The air had grown chilly and Gina felt grateful she'd worn her sweater. The evening air smelled fresh and clean, like damp soil.

The bed of monkshood stood out in the twilight only because the white, and bicolor blossoms glowed in the moonlight. The darker purple flowers were hidden by the lack of light.

"This is a lot of monkshood, isn't it?" he asked.

"I don't remember ever seeing an entire bed of it in anyone's garden. Then again, not that many people grow it. Probably because it's poisonous. It's a very beautiful flower though. And the fernlike leaves have a lovely texture. It's easy enough to grow."

The sheriff took out his flashlight and shone it around.

"Would they have used the root or the leaves?" asked Gina.

"I don't know. The coroner said all parts of it are poisonous. The seeds are too, but they would have had to use seeds from another year, right?"

"Well, the plants still have blooms. They haven't set this year's seeds yet."

"I can't see where there's been any digging to get roots. Can you?"

"No, but anyone in their right mind would have smoothed out to the soil. And they might have gotten roots a month ago, or even longer. Who knows? Do you know if the root or leaves have to be fresh or can be used dried to poison someone?"

"No idea. Can you see a place where an entire plant was taken?" asked the sheriff.

She squinted. It was difficult to see, since the purple flowers were almost invisible. Then she remembered a trick she'd learned from a garden designer, for finding gaps in garden beds. She took out her cell phone and opened the camera, turning on the flash. She took a photo of the entire bed and opened a photo editing app. She converted the photo to black and white, and noticed a gap between some plants.

She held the phone up and said, "There. Right between that white and bicolor one. There's a gap."

"Bicolor?" he asked.

"The purple and white one. Bi means two in latin."

He looked where she was pointing. Shone his flashlight on the soil.

"I see it," he said. "Look, there's a depression there, in the soil."

"So, there is a plant missing."

"Yes," he said. He took out his cell and stood at the edge of the bed, leaning over to get as close as possible, and taking several photos.

"Will the tests of the wine or port be able to tell what part of the plant was used? Does one part of the plant have less flavor and might be more easily masked by the port?"

"I don't know," he said. "That was a neat trick, the black and white thing. How did you learn it?"

"Some garden designers use it. It takes away the distraction of color so you can see the textures and shapes of a garden more clearly. Figure out what's missing, what needs to be added in or taken out to make a bed look more complete."

"The world never ceases to amaze me. Guess I need another app on my phone, huh?" he said.

"There's no end to that rabbit hole."

"Well, I guess that'll do till morning. Let me know if you find any more monkshood in your wanderings."

"I will. I need to get a map of this garden so I can figure out which sections I've missed. It's so complex."

"Is there a map of the garden?"

"Designers frequently make maps. I haven't met the gardener yet, but I'd really like to."

"I've met him. Briefly, before the coroner suggested aconite poisoning."

"Well, now you can have a more interesting conversation, I'd guess."

"What do you mean?" the sheriff asked.

He was messing with her. He had that gleam in his eye, testing her to see if she knew things he didn't.

"You could find out who strolls through the gardens and who doesn't. Who knows anything about plants? Who might have collected seeds or roots? Who might have walked in his pristine garden beds and when? That sort of thing."

"Yeah, you're right. Most of those were on my list. Not the pristine garden bed thing. Would he have noticed that?"

"I think so. From what I've seen. Now, the garden might just have been spruced up and made immaculate for the wedding, but it is pristine. Nothing out of place. Someone is cleaning it up almost 24/7. And the fact that they can do that tells me this garden has a long history of someone tidying up on a regular basis. I've not seen one weed yet. Not one faded flower. Not one broken stem. That doesn't happen in my garden, I can tell you and my tiny garden is fairly tidy. This garden is huge."

"Okay, after I come out in the morning and take more photos, I'll have a chat with the gardener again. Thank you. You've been a big help."

"You're welcome. Wish I could give you the name of the murderer."

"Got any bright ideas?"

"None at the moment. What did you find out about Tristan? I overheard Maggie having a conversation with someone out in the garden. It could have been the gardener. Tristan sounded like he was a horrible person."

"He was a mess. If you heard that he cheated everyone, then you heard correctly. On every deal it seems, and his employees, too. They all hated him. No one at his company is mourning his demise. His manager has a distant hope that he'll be left the company in his will. I doubt Tristan even had a will, he was so young. And the company has very little money. Any time it made money, Tristan siphoned it off to pay for something. Either paying himself an exorbitant bonus, or for office equipment or furnishings for his home office. Anything he could justify he did. Trips to Asia, that's where he did most of his business, it seems. And there were several women, other than Emma, who he bought expensive jewelry for. Then again, he often imported jewelry and somehow the company paid for his gifts. The manager was hacked off about that."

"Emma knew about at least one of them," said Gina. "We had a talk today."

"Did she? Well that should soften the blow then. I need to talk to her again, too. Did you learn anything interesting?"

"No. She's having a hard time with his death, feeling grief-stricken and angry all at once."

"Well, that's understandable, and interesting. Tristan's parents had no idea what he was up to. Both of them are in real estate, but Tristan didn't want to be part of the family business. His second year of business school, he struck out on his own. Creating his company."

"So, do you think it's possible someone snuck onto the island and killed him?"

"Possible, but highly unlikely. I'm still putting my money on someone who's here."

"An employee? Or future family?"

"That I don't know. I have candidates from each pool," the sheriff said.

They had reached the Japanese Garden which lay in full darkness now. There weren't even any solar lights or motion detector lights so common in large gardens. Did no one go outside at night around here? She should ask.

The sky was cloudy, so no stars were visible. The overcast skies glowed slightly giving a small amount of light, just enough to see to walk by. The air smelled moist, like it was about to rain.

Gina hoped it would rain tonight. Get the wetness out of its system by tomorrow. She didn't want to be cooped up inside. And she had only brought the wussy raincoat, not the heavy one. She'd only planned on staying two days at most. Maybe she could borrow one. The sheriff left her outside her room.

"Guess both the deputy and I will be staying the night. I want to be here when the sun comes up."

"Where is the deputy? I haven't seen him."

"He's discovered the kitchen."

"You'll never drag him out. The food is too good."

"I don't think he's there for the food."

Gina laughed.

"Well, goodnight. I'll see you tomorrow at some point," said the sheriff.

"Goodnight."

She went inside her room and took her sweater off. It was just the right temperature inside. She plugged her phone in to charge and noticed the time. 8:32 p.m.

It was still early, but she'd barely slept last night. Had she slept at all? She couldn't even remember. Which meant she desperately needed sleep now.

FRIDAY MORNING

The next morning she woke to sun streaming in her window and making the room warm and toasty. Gina had been so tired last night, she'd forgotten to close the curtains. The clock by her bed said it was 7:30 a.m.

She sat on the edge of the bed trying to remember what day it was. And couldn't.

It probably didn't matter. She was here until the sheriff let them go.

She gave a deep sigh and breathed in the scent of lilacs from her bedside bouquet. Then stood and went to the bathroom. Her short hair stood on end in an unseemly fashion. No amount of water on her brush was going to fix that. She needed a shower.

As she soaped up a random thought came to her.

Had the gardener known Tristan? Was there some history there that no one knew about?

Since she'd never even seen the gardener Gina had no clue about any of that. Tristan's business had mostly taken him to

Asia, the sheriff said. And the gardener had a European accent. But perhaps they had met. Or perhaps the gardener knew one of the women Tristan was dating.

She should talk to the sheriff about it today.

If the sheriff hadn't left last night, then that meant the Matthews were still here. She glanced at the clock. 8:30. Maybe they'd already eaten. They looked like early risers. And they still might be on eastern time, which was three hours ahead.

She dressed and slipped her cell phone into the pocket of her jacket and left the room. She'd grab a quick breakfast. Maybe Maggie would be there and Gina could ask about a map of the garden.

Gina had lots of photos she needed take to paint from. And she had to see if there was monkshood elsewhere in the garden. She also needed to find the compost area and see if there was any discarded monkshood there.

In the dining room sat Maggie, Jennifer and Marsha. They were sitting close to each other, whispering and giggling. Gina walked in and they glanced up quickly, became stone faced, then looked relieved when they saw it was her.

"I didn't mean to interrupt," said Gina.

Jennifer said, "It's not you. We were being rude about Maggie's guests. Her other guests."

"Oh, those guests," said Gina.

"Honestly," said Maggie. "Last night was the worst dinner I've ever been at, let alone hosted. I'm so sorry."

"The food was spectacular," said Gina.

She poured a cup of steaming, hot water and dunked a teabag of Irish breakfast tea into it.

"You know, I don't think Tiffany has ever made a bad meal.

And those other two women, they're smoking, too. We might have to bribe them to stay," said Maggie.

Gina lifted the silver lid off a platter on the buffet. Beneath it sat several fresh cinnamon rolls. The dough was darker than cinnamon rolls she was used to, too dark to be whole wheat. They had white icing.

"Are these chocolate?" Gina asked in amazement.

"Yup. Chocolate cinnamon rolls. Julie's recipe," said Jennifer. "And they are awesome. You're lucky I haven't eaten them all. I bailed after four of them."

"I only had two," said Marsha.

Gina dished up two. She added a piece of ham so she'd at least get some protein to balance out the sugar.

She sat across from Jennifer and Marsha, and next to Maggie.

Biting into a cinnamon roll, she tasted the gooey, buttery chocolate dough. And the cinnamon. It was incredibly decadent.

"Oh my god," Gina said, once she'd swallowed.

They all laughed.

"So where have the Matthews gone?" Gina asked, taking the teabag out of her tea and squeezing it over the cup, then depositing the finished bag on her saucer. She reached for the cream and splashed a bit in the tea.

"Paul's showing them around. They ate breakfast much, much earlier. The Sheriff's taking them back to the mainland after lunch," Maggie said, making a scrunched up face.

"I think it's a good day for a picnic," Jennifer said to Marsha.

"You're on. We can hike to the lookout and eat there," said Marsha.

"I don't wanna hike," wailed Jennifer.

"We both need the exercise. Especially those of us who ate four cinnamon rolls," said Marsha.

Gina managed to eat the ham and three cinnamon rolls. She felt stuffed, but the cinnamon rolls were so good, she couldn't stop eating them. Maggie and Jennifer baited each other like a couple of kids. It was very good-natured and funny.

Deputy Hofsteader came in the dining room door, nodded and said, "Good morning ladies." His crew cut had grown a bit since she'd last seen him, giving him a little curl in those blond locks. He still looked boyish even with his size.

"What can I do for you?" asked Maggie.

"I was just on my way to the kitchen," he said, his face pinking up a bit.

"Don't leave without trying some of those cinnamon rolls," said Jennifer, laughing.

"She's on a sugar high," said Maggie, explaining to the deputy.

"I don't know if I can eat any more of the great food those ladies cook. I had so many cookies yesterday that I had to run six miles this morning."

"Where did you run?" asked Marsha.

"Around and around and around. Every road I could find and then out in the garden. I scared some poor rabbit half to death."

"Dustin will be pleased with that. He's declared war on the rabbits. Someone brought in a couple of pregnant ones, decades ago. They've overrun the island. There's so few predators here. We have a few hawks, sometimes an eagle. Maybelle catches a few. Ninja might catch some as well. Max never does. He hangs out by the kitchen and waits for Tiffany to feed him, lazy bugger," said Maggie.

"So, there's three cats?" asked Gina. "I met Maybelle last night. And the black one is Ninja, I'm guessing? What color is Max?"

"Maximillian is an orange tiger cat. The king of all he surveys. He's quite friendly. Especially if you've got meat. Lovely cat, though," said Maggie.

During their conversation the deputy had nodded and continued on to the kitchen.

"Say, is there a map of the garden?" asked Gina. "I keep getting lost and I know I'm missing parts of it."

"You know, I don't know. Dustin designed it. Let's go hunt him down after breakfast and ask. I've been wanting to introduce you, but I keep forgetting. And I've been busy with the Matthews." Maggie rolled her eyes.

"That would be wonderful. I don't want to miss any bit of it. Every part of the garden that I've seen has been more wonderful and surprising than the last. It's quite remarkable."

"Thank you. And Dustin will be pleased to hear that."

"Is he the only one who works on it?"

"I do sometimes, not a great deal. And he does all the big stuff. We used to have people come in to do the hardscaping: brick laying, large sculptures, arbors, those sorts of things. That was years ago. But now all that stuff is done. I think Dustin would love to have someone come do some of the maintenance, so he could carve out more territory. He's contenting himself with reworking some of the older beds. He's been buying plants like crazy all spring. And itching to get them into the ground. Since there's no wedding, I told him to have at it. At least someone can be happy. He was so disappointed the wedding was cancelled. He worked so hard to make the garden perfect for it," said Maggie.

"And it is perfect, I'm amazed at how tidy everything is," said Gina.

After breakfast, Maggie led her out a door in the parlor. The air was still crisp, but the day promised warmth.

Outside the parlor, the garden was loaded with hybrid rhodies in full bloom. It was a rainbow of colors. About a third of the plants were rhodies. Another third were summer blooming shrubs like *Weigela,* roses and *Hydrangea.* Gina spotted a mock orange that had yellowish-lime green leaves with white flowers. Its sweet scent she caught clear across that section of the garden.

The last third of the plants were perennials and bulbs. There were a lot of *Heuchera,* with light purple mottled leaves, and many Japanese painted ferns.

Small-flowered *Anemone* covered much of the ground. The nickel-sized white, pastel yellow, pink and lavender blossoms looked very cheery. Gina knew they would fade as summer began. What would replace them? Clearly seeing this garden in spring was just the beginning.

The path curved around a bed of conifers ranging from forty feet tall to the smallest dwarf ones which stood only a couple of inches high. The colors were varied from deep emerald green to blue to yellow-green. There were a couple of variegated conifers in the bed too. The textures of the plants were just as varied.

Then the path curved again and there stood a man in front of a completely bare bed. He had a large cart completely filled with plants in black pots and looked to be trying to decide what to put where.

"Oh Dustin, how are you doing? Looks like you've made great progress," said Maggie.

The man, who had a full head of brown hair, looked to be in his forties. He smiled and his face wrinkled when he did it. The smile went all the way to his eyes. He was quite a handsome, healthy looking guy.

"Good morning, Maggie. I'm grand this lovely morning. You know I've been itchin' to tear this bed up for years."

"I know," said Maggie.

Gina saw with a shock that it was the bed that had been filled with monkshood just last night, the tall bamboo forest stood in the background. She felt like someone had punched her in the stomach.

Had the sheriff come out this morning and taken photos? She sure hoped so.

Maggie grabbed Gina's arm and pulled her over near the cart.

"This is Gina Wetherby, the painter. Gina this is Dustin Keane. He's our estate manager and gardener."

"Ah, 'tis lovely to meet you. I've seen your paintings in the house. You do a remarkable job of capturing the life of plants. It's an honor," he said, grinning and pulling his gloves off, then holding out his hand.

Gina shook his hand. It took her a moment to recover her senses and be polite. Surely this man couldn't be a murderer?

"It's an honor to meet you too. This garden is one of the most stunning I've ever seen."

"Well, thank you. I love this place. The range of plants we're able to grow here is so large. It's a great deal of fun."

"Gina was wondering if you have a map of the gardens. She doesn't want to miss anything."

"I do, actually. It's in the tool shed. It's not exactly up to date. Something's always changing. If you'd like to see it now, I can show you."

"I'd like that," said Gina.

Maggie nodded.

They followed him down another curving path, that threaded through sections Gina hadn't seen before, until they reached what must have been the edge of the garden. Beyond lay a forest of madrona, big-leaf maple and behind them, tall cedar trees.

In front of the stand of native trees stood a green wooden building with a slanted, flat roof and three large windows. Dustin opened the front door and walked inside. They followed him into the medium-sized room. Three walls were lined with large tools hanging on hooks or small ones neatly arranged on shelves. There was a heavy, battered wooden table in the middle of the room. Made to stand at, the top was at waist level and had large plastic bins beneath it, labeled potting soil, seed starting mix and carnivorous plant mix. Several black plastic pots lay on top of the table. A stack of plant labels sat nearby, ready for action. The floor of the building was concrete.

Dustin switched on a light and led them over to one wall where a large, once folded, paper hung on a cork board. It looked like the garden designs she'd seen by professional designers. There were smaller sheets of paper—8x10 size, stuck all around the larger one, seemingly for individual garden beds. They looked very intricate.

"This is the main map," he said, pointing to the large paper. It had been drawn on with pencil and written on, much erased and redrawn.

It showed the garden wrapping around the house. The outer perimeters formed a U-shape around the house. The uprights of the U had their own internal patterns that curved and swirled into spirals. The bottom of the U formed a line behind which another entire pattern evolved. One which mirrored the shape of the house. So if one saw it from the air, there would have been a sun formed by the house, and a full moon formed by that section of the garden. The moon bed also divided up into a half moon and a crescent moon.

Gina also noticed that there was a garden area on the other side of the driveway. So, more territory to explore. These were labeled: the Chinese garden, the English garden and the Italian garden. They connected to the Japanese garden on the map. She hadn't even noticed that, so intent on the garden surrounding the back side of the house.

Just looking at all of it, she felt exhausted. How was she ever going to see it all?

"How can you possibly take care of all this?" she asked.

"I don't sleep," he said, laughing.

"No, really."

"It's a labor of love. It's not work to me. Paul's given me this entire island as a canvas. I'm sure you can appreciate how exciting and what a challenge it is. How much fun I'm having. I won't be able to do it forever. And there are some days I think we should hire some extra help. But that would cut into my plant budget," he grinned again.

"He really is remarkable," said Maggie.

"Do you have another copy of this map?" asked Gina.

"I don't. But if you promise to bring it back, you can take this one while you walk around the garden."

"Oh, I couldn't do that," said Gina.

"Sure you could. You're not going to leave the island today that's for sure. I think the Sheriff's going to keep everyone here until he solves the murder. You might as well walk around and know where you are. Provided you can interpret my scrawling."

"It's clear to me," said Gina, watching him take out the push pins and remove the map from the wall. "I can see the pattern you've made. Very clever. I like the way you've mirrored the sun with the moon of the garden."

"I'm glad you caught that. It took Maggie years to notice. I originally wanted to do the moon garden with a pond, then I realized the koi would be happier in the glasshouse. Where they can eat all year round."

"It's better for the guests too. They can go visit them in the winter and when it's pouring down rain outside," said Maggie.

"That's true," Dustin said. "So we built the roof from the house to the glasshouse so people can go outside even when there are torrential downpours."

"And the glasshouse is so lovely in our dark, gloomy winters," said Maggie. "I often go out there and sit with a cup of cocoa, with peppermint schnapps in it. It's so cozy to be inside and warm, listening to the rain pounding down and surrounded by a jungle of tropical beauty."

"I can imagine," said Gina.

She could almost smell the damp soil, the sweet scent of blooming jasmine, and other tropicals on a gray January day.

"So you keep the greenhouse heated all winter?" Gina asked.

"We let the temperature dip a bit in December and January. Just enough to let the koi go semi-dormant. Just in case they ever need to go into an outside pond, they'll be able to survive. And who knows what will happen in the future? We have generators on the greenhouse, to keep the pump going and the heat running in case we lose power, but if the system breaks down completely for some reason, we want the koi to be able to survive."

Gina nodded. What would it take for the whole system to break down long enough that the generators might run out of gas?

"Are you in danger of flooding because of climate change?"

"We'll lose the docks and everything down near the water. Mostly, it depends on how much of a sea level rise we get here. The house and other dwellings are up on the top of the island. It's a good possibility they'll stay dry, but maybe not," he shrugged. As if saying no one really knew.

"We do worry about that," said Maggie. "Paul especially. We'll probably both be gone, of course, but Emma won't be and neither will this garden. It's such a shame. I don't think about it much, because I get so angry at the world that it makes me want to murder corporation heads and so-called leaders. How could all of them, how could we, let the world get in such a state?"

"A long history of corruption," said Gina, "and very little accountability. With a huge helping of disconnection from nature."

She was getting too warm and slipped her jacket off, tying the sleeves around her waist.

"That's very true," said Dustin. "So many people who live in large cities only see nature in the form of a single tree in a park. Not as a forest of interconnected beings who nurture each other. They have no understanding of how nature works and they don't care." Duncan refolded the map until it was about 8" x 4", then handed the map to Gina.

"Thank you," said Gina. "I'll bring it back, promise."

"I've no doubts. If I'm not here, just leave it on the table. Sometimes, I'm hard to find," said Duncan.

"Well," said Maggie, "I should get back to the house. My mother, grandmother and aunt are all in Everett, waiting for the Sheriff to let them come over or for him to pick them up. And Paul's relations are still coming today, for support. And Sheila needs some help getting everything ready. Gayle's still a mess after finding Tristan."

"Oh?" said Gina.

"She was really shaken up. She's only eighteen and had never seen anyone die. She's working, but slowly, and Sheila keeps finding her sitting around gazing off into the distance. Forgetting what she was supposed to do. I don't know what to do about it. The girl got dumped by her first boyfriend a year or so back and I don't think she ever grieved for that loss. Gayle told Tiffany that Tristan reminded her of her old boyfriend. I think she's grieving for that old relationship now."

"Poor kid," said Dustin.

"I'll walk back with you," said Gina. "I'd like to get rid of my jacket before I launch into taking a bunch of photos."

Walking back to the house Maggie led Gina through parts of the garden she began to recognize. Some of the sections she had seen her first evening on the island. The sunny border filled with foxgloves, hardy *Geranium* and *Viburnum*. Smack in the middle of the bed was a clump of the bicolor monkshood. She'd seen them and not remembered. They blended in so well with the rest of the bed, she'd only seen them as part of the whole. Some of the stalks had been ripped off about halfway up.

Dustin wouldn't have done that. He would have cut them off at the base.

Gina couldn't see him as a murderer, no matter that he had easy access to the poison and probably the knowledge that monkshood was poisonous.

The sun came out from behind a cloud making her feel nice and toasty.

"Oh, I love it when the sun shines. I'm a transplant and although I love it here, I do have problems with all the gray and darkness," said Maggie.

"And I can't even imagine what it's like to have spent so long planning a wedding only to have everything fall apart when the groom was murdered. And then be descended on by more houseguests," said Gina.

"It's heartbreaking," said Maggie. "No matter how much I disliked Tristan, my heart breaks for Emma. I think she'll turn out okay, but I wish I could take away her pain."

"We always do, don't we?"

"You have children, I'm guessing," said Maggie.

"Three daughters, all grown now."

"And you still worry about them?" asked Maggie.

"I don't think that part ever ends. My daughters left home more than a decade ago and I still worry. Even though I really do understand they're doing well. They're all so different and their paths in life are all very different. Sometimes I worry that I'm responsible for that and that they're all rebelling against what I did with my life," said Gina.

"Rebelling how?"

"One of my daughters travels the world, then works her

tail off to earn as much money as fast as she can, then she's off traveling again. Another works as a mask maker in Hollywood. She never raises her head up and looks around to see that there's anything else to life other than work. The other is back east with a high-paying job. She and her husband are very much into piling up money. I don't think a one of my daughters has ever though about having kids. I'm not upset about that. Honestly, I'm not one of those women who lives for the possibility of future grandchildren. I just wish that all of them would look around and see that there's more to life than money. Well Shelly sees that. She lives to travel, but that means so much of her life is lost to working and it's like she's living a half life. I just want them all to feel like their life is full and complex and well-lived on all levels."

"I understand. I never gave much thought to money when I was single. I worked in an art gallery and paid my rent and that was just fine. Then when I was twenty-five, Paul waltzed into the gallery and left with three very expensive paintings. And my heart. I guess I haven't had to think about money. I've been very lucky to have the luxury to just live," said Maggie.

"You have been lucky, and you aren't spoiled about it either."

"Oh, I am spoiled though. I have three cooks. Who I'm trying to convince that they'd really love to live here and work!

"That's it, I'm leaving my house and moving in," said Gina.

"Oh, I wish you would! We could have so much fun together. Paul is fun sometimes, but most times he's got his mind on business and he's a stick in the mud. So Sheila and I make up theme nights and we party. Taco Tuesdays, Wacky Wednesdays, Frog Fridays. We create elaborate costumes, collect appropriate music and have a dance. Sometimes, the other staff deign to join us. Sheila and I are easily amused."

"It sounds like fun," said Gina.

"So you want to come live here? Room and board free. Oh, and an amazing garden to paint?"

"It's tempting. Oh so tempting. But my cats would be devastated. And I do have friends on the Raven Island."

"You can bring your cats. And your friends. No? Well then, you'll just have to come visit. A lot. Because the garden changes so much, not just with the seasons. It changes daily. And bring your friends when you come. The more the merrier."

"I just might have to take you up on that," said Gina. "I'd love to see this garden at other times of the year. And I do love tacos."

Gina realized Maggie was lonely. She was so outgoing, living here on the island must certainly put a cramp in her socializing. Coming over to visit would be fun. Provided Maggie, Paul or Emma weren't the murderer.

They were back at the house before Gina realized it.

Maggie went off to the offices to make phone calls, and Gina returned to her room to get rid of her jacket. She lay it on the bed, thinking it might be needed this evening.

Then drank a glass of tap water, which must come from a well. Or would any well water here be salt water? Gina didn't know, but she did notice the water didn't have a chlorine flavor and tasted fresh and clean. She hated the chemical tang of chlorine.

Her phone buzzed and she pulled it out of the jacket pocket. Melanie.

Gina said, "Hello."

"Hi Gina. I haven't heard from you and wanted to make sure you're still alive."

"I am, but wow have things gotten complicated."

Gina walked out into the main room of the suite and opened the large glass doors. She went outside and sat on the metal chair at the cafe table on her patio.

Someone, probably Dustin, had added two huge containers to the patio. One, contained a citrus tree of some sort in full bloom. The small white flowers had a strong, sweet scent that wafted across the patio to her. The other container held a large, peach colored New Zealand flax, variegated *Pelargonium* that had gaudy peach, maroon and green leaves and several trailing annuals she couldn't name, that had maroon flowers.

The sun shone down on the patio, making it feel warm.

"What have you done now?" asked Melanie.

"I haven't done anything, but the groom has been murdered."

"You're still on Frost Island? I thought you were coming back yesterday. I didn't hear from you, so I assumed you'd found another ride home."

"I'm still here," said Gina. She filled Melanie in on the details.

"So, you have no idea when you get to leave. Bummer. How's Shelly doing?"

"She sounds fine. Tired, but she discovered Corr's and their chocolate cake."

"I'll have to drop by and say hello. Make sure she can find everything she needs. Like all the good restaurants in town."

"That would be great. Although, I suspect she's broke. If you take her out for a meal, I'll pay you back."

"No you won't! I'm a working woman and I can pay for another poor woman's meal these days," said Melanie, with mock indignance.

Gina laughed.

"Your choice."

"It'd be fun to take her out. I'll make her tell me stories about her travels in return for food. I like to travel, but vicariously. Not so much fun to stand in line at airport or train stations and eat bad food. Sleeping in lumpy beds is not my thing."

"I hear you. Not mine either. Not anymore anyway. I miss my cats."

"You mean on that ritzy island they don't have any cats?"

"Apparently, there are three. I glimpsed a black one, had a nice chat with a lovely tabby last night. Haven't seen the yellow one yet. But this garden Melanie, you have to see it. It's one of the most amazing gardens I've ever seen."

"Really?"

"Really. It's stunning. The plant combinations, the design. Wow."

"What's the most exotic thing you've seen there?"

Melanie was a propagator at Ravenswood Nursery. She knew her plants.

"Well, I don't know. They have a huge glasshouse of tropicals, with a koi pond. There's probably some really exotic plants in there. I saw a gorgeous *Arisaema*, and oodles of fawn and trout lilies. Oh, and Tasmanian tree ferns."

"I do love me some Tasmanian tree ferns."

"I haven't even been through most of the gardens yet. There's a huge patch that's a timber bamboo forest. Like the ones you see in photos from Japan."

"Oh my."

"And the food is incredible. I need to leave before I can't fit into my clothes anymore."

"Okay, okay. Tell me when and I'll see if I can come with you next time. After the murderer is caught."

"That can't come soon enough for me."

Gina heard knocking at her door inside, so she got up and went inside to answer it. It was the Sheriff.

"The Sheriff's here. I'll call you when I need a ride, okay?"

"I'll be here. Watch out for that man. I think he's sweet on you."

"Not likely. See ya."

Why would Melanie say such a thing? She couldn't be serious. The Sheriff didn't have a personal life. How could he?

Gina clicked off the phone.

"Hi," Gina said to him.

"Good morning. I need to talk to you."

"Come on in. I was just sitting out on the patio."

"I'd like to sit down. Maybe my brain would stop spinning in circles," he said.

They went outside and sat down.

She said, "I was thinking last night. Wondering if there was some sort of connection between Tristan and the gardener. Then I met the gardener this morning and I can't see him being a murderer."

"Why?" asked the sheriff.

"Well, when I met him, he had just pulled up the entire patch of monkshood and was getting ready to replant the area with a cartload of new plants. That made me think he was guilty. Then Maggie and I talked to him for awhile. The more we did, the less I thought it was possible. Then when Maggie and I walked back to the house we went through a part of the garden I had seen on my first day here. There's a clump of monkshood there. With several stalks torn off, halfway up the stem. Dustin wouldn't have done that. He would have cut them back at the base. One to avoid detection, two to make it tidy."

"I know which section you're talking about. I found it myself this morning and noticed the ripped stems. However, Dustin might have done it if he was trying to implicate someone else."

"Possibly."

"I went out early this morning and walked around the entire garden," said the sheriff. "I only found monkshood in those two places. None in the compost bins or the burn pile. When I talked to Dustin this morning, as he was pulling up all the plants, he said the plant that had been in the hole we noticed had gone missing a couple of weeks ago. He noticed it at the time, but didn't do anything about it, because he figured no one else would notice it missing. And he was busy trying to clean up for the wedding and get everything looking good. He couldn't figure out who or what would have taken it or why. There aren't any deer, cows or grazing animals on the island. Then, after Tristan was killed and poison had been confirmed, he put things together. Decided to pull all the monkshood from everywhere in the garden and compost it all. He feels responsible for growing a plant that killed someone," said the sheriff. "Figures if Maggie and Paul find out they'll sack him."

"I think that's unlikely. Do you believe him?"

"I don't know. I haven't decided whether he's the most honest man I've ever met, or if he's an amazingly, gifted liar."

"I sort of believe him, but then I'm not the best judge of character."

"And he's handsome and charming."

"Handsome never did much for me, and he's just a kid. I simply admire that he's so dedicated to his work." Gina laughed. "And here I've been going on all morning to Maggie, and Melanie, about two of my daughters living for their jobs. Silly me."

"Well, we're all biased as to what we see."

"Are there any other suspects?"

"I'm still thinking about Paul. I'm still trying to see if there's any disgruntled employees. Then again, I'm wondering how much he disliked his daughter's choice of fiancé."

"There is that," said Gina.

Her stomach rumbled. Loudly.

"I heard that," said the sheriff. He glanced at his watch. "It's lunchtime. I need to decide whether it's safe to let all those relatives come over. I don't feel like letting anyone off the island yet. Are you doing all right?"

"I'm good. I've got food, a beautiful garden to photograph and paint. It feels like I'm on vacation. Except for the part about a murderer being on the loose."

"I'm stuck on that, I have to admit."

"Have you found any disgruntled employees?"

"Not a one. Everyone seems to love Paul and Maggie. They appear to be the fairest employers anyone has ever had. The only complaint people have is that working here is remote. They can't go out and party with their friends every night, even though they can on their weekends off. They also said the tradeoff is worth it. So far, that's a dead-end."

"Unless it's not an employee who might have tried to kill Paul, and got Tristan instead."

"I've checked and checked family members. Maggie's clean

so far as I can tell. So are Jennifer and Marsha. Emma seems to be. Paul is a hard man to pin down. I can't find that there's any reason someone would have wanted him dead. He's a successful businessman. Someone would have wanted to kill him. You don't get through life at his level of success without that. But, it doesn't seem to be family. I keep coming back to someone from the outside wanting to kill Paul and getting Tristan. Or someone, perhaps Paul, perhaps not, wanting to kill Tristan."

"And you've ruled out suicide?"

"No one in their right mind would choose that method for suicide. Aconite poisoning is a terrible way to die. Hours and hours of horrible pain before death. Nope. Suicides generally choose faster-acting methods. And I've found no reason he wanted to die. He cheated everyone, but there was still money coming in. He was about to be married to a beautiful wealthy woman, who he was also cheating on."

"Okay. I'll keep my ears open still. I'll try to talk to Paul. See if I can find out where he really stood on the marriage."

"Better do it soon. I can't hold off the relatives much longer. Some people run away from crisis. Others descend on the family and try to make everything better. I think both of these families are descenders."

"I'll do it after lunch then," said Gina.

"Lunch. Let's go find lunch," said the sheriff. "I'm starving. And I need to tell Hofsteader to take the boat over to the mainland and pick everyone up. He'll love that. He always wants to drive." Sheriff Jansson grinned.

They went back inside her room and she closed the glass doors. She grabbed her jacket, mainly because it had a pocket large enough for the map. And her phone. She planned on escaping the lunch table as soon as possible and going outside. Hopefully catching Paul alone, but avoiding the Matthews as much as possible.

"Thanks for talking to me," he said. "You always help me clear my mind."

"You're welcome. I'm glad I could help."

"You know, you should've been a detective," he said.

"No. I can think my way through things, but chasing down suspects? No way."

He laughed and opened the door to the hallway.

When they got to the dining room, the Matthews, Maggie and Paul were there, already seated and drinking coffee.

Sheriff Jansson said to the Matthews, "I'll see that the deputy takes you back to the mainland after lunch."

"Oh, thank you," said Mrs. Matthews.

Mr. Matthews said nothing, just sat stone-faced.

The sheriff turned to Maggie and Paul and said, "He'll also pick up your relatives and bring them over."

"Oh good," said Paul. "Thank you. I'll call them."

"Could you call Elizabeth and let her know?" Maggie asked Paul.

"Will do. I'll be right back. Start eating without me, please."

Paul got up and left the room.

The sheriff went into the kitchen and Gina could hear him good-naturedly haranguing the deputy about hanging around in the kitchen.

FRIDAY AFTERNOON

I t wasn't long before Tiffany came out to take their orders. Gina chose a grilled cheese sandwich and iced tea.

When it came, she discovered the cheese included goat, cheddar and gruyere cheeses. The cooks had also added arugula and mustard greens to the sandwich, which added some bite to complement the richness of the cheese. It was the best grilled cheese she'd ever had. On a light rye bread which had been baked earlier in the day.

The iced tea was basically black tea to which lemon balm had been added during the brewing. Delicious.

Mrs. Matthews seemed almost giddy, probably at the prospect of leaving. Gina got the impression that it had been Mr. Matthew's idea to come here and make the Frosts feel guilty for the death of their son.

What horrible pain he must be in. She felt sorry for him. He had probably been that way his entire life. She'd known people like him when she'd worked in marketing. They were awful to be around. A human black hole of emotion, they sucked all the life out of a room, and all the joy.

Emma didn't show up for lunch. When Paul came back from telephoning, he asked where she was.

"Has anyone seen her all day?" he asked.

"Leave her alone," said Maggie. "She wants to be alone."

He clearly didn't agree. Gina figured he'd go look for her after lunch. She'd have to be quick if she wanted to talk to him.

And just how would she go about that? Ask him if anyone wanted to kill him? Ask him if he'd hated Tristan, and would rather see Tristan dead before he married Paul's daughter?

She couldn't think of a tactful way of going about it. But his relatives would be coming as soon as the deputy delivered the Matthews to the mainland. Right after lunch. When they came, Gina felt sure his time would be spoken for.

Gina asked, "Whose idea was the separate gardens across the driveway?"

"Mine," said Paul.

"Why China, England and Italy?"

"Well, Maggie and I went to Italy for our honeymoon, the gardens were beautiful. And I've always liked those formal English gardens. As for China, when I was younger my parents took me to China with them. I remember seeing a few of the gardens that hadn't been torn apart by the revolution. They fascinated me. They were so exotic with their massive limestone rocks. Most of the exotic plants won't grow here, of course. Dustin tells me we're too cold. Same with Italy. But he's done a wonderful job of replicating the look and using those plants that will thrive in our climate."

"Could you show me around there?" asked Gina. "I haven't been over there."

"Then how do you know about them?"

"I have a map," she said, patting the folded map in the pocket of her jacket, hanging on her chair.

"A map? Where did you get that?" Paul asked, his face lighting up in wonder.

"Dustin."

"Of course. Of course Dustin would make a map. The man never ceases to surprise me. You're on. I'd love to give you a tour, because you'll need to paint over there. There are some Chinese tree peonies over there still in bloom, I think. They are spectacular. But better get to them quickly. Tree peonies seem to be one of those flowers—here today, gone tomorrow," said Paul.

"You're right about that," said Gina, "but even when they're fading, they make beautiful paintings. Just a different mood."

They continued eating. Gina was prepared to refuse dessert until the chefs brought out three silver trays of petit fours. Little bite sized cakes, each covered with a stiff frosting and decorated with tiny frosted flowers. The frosting and cakes came in vanilla, lemon and chocolate. The cooks were solidly into serving the wedding food now.

Gina had to try one of each. And then another round. She couldn't tell which she liked the best. She usually wasn't a lemon fan, but the little cakes were so buttery that it mellowed out the tartness of the lemon somewhat.

She sipped her iced tea and tried to match personalities to flavor. Mr. Matthews was definitely lemon. Maggie was chocolate. Paul seemed to like all of them. Mrs. Matthews was distinctly vanilla.

Gina couldn't pinpoint exactly why she disliked the Matthews so much. Partly, it was their need to make Maggie and Paul feel guilty. Otherwise, why come over to the island when all their business with Tristan's funeral must be on the mainland? Other than the kind greeting they'd given Emma yesterday, they hadn't seemed to be there for her. Gina hadn't heard them mention her and they had looked unconcerned earlier when Paul asked about Emma.

She also didn't like their snobbery. Nothing seemed good enough for them and they'd made it clear they didn't really want to be here. She'd be very glad to see the back of them.

After dessert they left to go get their luggage.

Gina breathed a sigh of relief when they left the room. She wasn't the only one. Maggie looked so relieved.

"Where are Jennifer and Marsha?" asked Gina.

"Picnic. Remember?"

"Oh, that's right. They missed the petit fours then."

"What a pity," said Maggie, taking another chocolate one. "I'll have to have another one for them."

Deputy Hofsteader came out of the kitchen and said, "Tell the Matthews that I'll be down at the docks."

Paul asked, "Do you need a ride?"

"No. I need the exercise. I've been eating too much good food," he said, grinning. Then left the room, going down the hallway towards the front door.

"Poor man, I can't tell which one he has a crush on. I hope none of them are going to run away with him," said Paul, nodding towards the kitchen.

"What?" asked Maggie.

"Haven't you noticed how much time he's been spending in the kitchen?"

"I thought it was the food," said Maggie.

"I know you did," said Paul, kissing her on the cheek.

"That's just one of the reasons I love you. You always think the best of everyone."

He stood up, "Shall we go tour the gardens?"

"I can't go," said Maggie. "Someone should see them off."

"Martin can see them off. They've been nothing but rude since they arrived. I really don't give a damn what they think of us."

"I should go help Sheila. Relatives coming."

"Okay, we'll see you when we get back," he said.

Gina grabbed another chocolate petit four and followed him out into the hallway.

They ran into Martin on the way to the front door and Paul asked him to drive the Matthews down to the dock. Martin nodded.

Had the sheriff seriously considered Martin as a suspect? Because the butler always did it. And Martin was very, very sharp. She'd have to ask the sheriff later.

Paul and Gina walked across the circular drive and began with the Italian garden. It was formal with most of the formality coming from the stonework. Pillars, tiled walkways and a rectangular pool of clear water. They must have used an algaecide in it and cleaned it on a regular basis. Of course, not a leaf floated in it.

The stone was all warm colored, mostly a pale yellow-tan. There were also paths off the main one, that were covered in a warm tan-colored gravel. The central area was all laid with pavers. Everything was frighteningly symmetrical.

Gina didn't like gardens quite that perfect.

Each corner of a bed was accented with identical two foot tall boxwoods pruned into cone shapes with points on top. At the end of each of the four paths sat huge terra cotta-colored containers, each filled with sweetly scented blooming citrus trees. Pruned so that they all looked identical. Two of the main beds were filled with lavender. They were far enough along in blooming that it was clear they'd been in the greenhouse until recently. Lavender around here didn't normally bloom until July.

The other two beds held large, well-pruned rosemary plants in full bloom. In the center of each bed stood a small bay tree. There were several statues of nearly naked gods and goddesses throughout the garden. They looked as if they were made of marble. Was that possible? The cost must have been exorbitant.

This garden was all about the tight control of nature. It made her very uncomfortable. It was too perfect. Too human-made.

Gina followed Paul through a nearly hidden exit behind one of the terra cotta containers. The path had the same tan gravel and wove between drooping deciduous trees, she couldn't identify. It ended near a massive, gray structure the size of a small delivery truck. It looked like a cave, except that every inch of it was covered with shells, matched by color and size. And elaborate mosaic. Most of them were from clams and mussels, although there were oyster shells and limpets too. It must have taken a phenomenal amount of work. Inside the cave was a bench made of the same material and a small dripping fountain that ended in a little pool. There were a couple of holes in the ceiling and side, which let in a bit of light. Feathery ferns dripped in through them.

"Who made this?" she asked, awestruck.

"I hired a company to create it. The rock is actually manmade and the shells were imbedded into it. It took a lot of time and a lot of layers of material. I'm really pleased with how it turned out. And of course, Dustin had to plant it. The ferns add a great touch."

"Wow. Every time I think I've seen the best of this garden, I turn around and there's something more amazing."

"Good. I wanted people to feel wonder at our amazing garden. I love the whole thing, but this is one of my favorite places. When things get too hectic I come out here and listen to the water dripping."

They went back to the path which continued on to the English garden. The gravel changed to gray, the normal color of gravel in the majority of local gardens Gina was familiar with. They went through an archway created in an immaculately pruned laurel hedge. The hedge bordered the entire garden.

Gina glanced around and recognized it immediately. This was the English garden, only a bit less formal than the Italian one.

The same hedge ran down the far side of the garden. In front of the hedge on both sides lay deep rectangular beds filled with perennials. Most of them were still quite short as it was early in the season.

Large antique rose bushes sprawled throughout the beds. Not flowering, but budded out. They looked different from the modern roses. Old roses were often once-blooming, their spectacular show lasting for a month or more, often followed by rose hips. They weren't cut back to a foot or two tall like most modern roses, but the canes generally left long with flowers blooming for most of the length.

Clematis twined around their legs. Ready to shoot up and put on a second show once the roses were fading.

Gina could see *Phlox*, blue *Delphinium*, foxgloves and a host of other taller perennials towards the back of the beds. In front of those stood bleeding hearts in full bloom. In the middle here were also modern rose plants, drowsy pink, red and white peonies and hardy *Geranium*. Gina could smell the sweetness of the peonies. Seedlings of hollyhocks, poppies and love-in-a-mist were scattered throughout the middle sections. Small species tulips, creeping *Phlox* and lily of the valley bordered the center walkway which was green grass, immaculate and cut short.

At this time of year, bare ground was visible, but in a month as the plants expanded it would disappear. The borders would be chock full of color. Gina didn't recognize all the plants. Many weren't in bloom yet. In a month this garden would be in its prime. Gina hoped she'd be able to come back and see it.

"It's really a shame there isn't going to be a wedding," she said. "Your garden deserves an audience."

"It's probably all for the best," said Paul. "I was willing to go along with it. Knowing Tristan was a cad. And that months, maybe years down the road, Emma would be heartbroken. I hate to say this, I'm relieved it ended now. A bad ending, but I don't think a good ending years later would have been possible."

"What do you mean, a cad?" asked Gina.

"You know the type, a womanizer. And his business practices were foolish. You don't drain all the profit off your business for long and survive. Some maybe, but all? That's just foolish. You need to keep putting it back into the business and helping it grow. I also didn't like the way he treated people who were his equals. I can't imagine how he treated his employees. He wasn't a good man. It's common these days, but I always think that sort of behavior will come back around and bite you. Then again, I've seen lots of people who seem to get away with it."

"It doesn't make it right," said Gina.

"No it doesn't. I would've chosen a better man for my daughter, but he was her choice, and how far can you push those things? We've always wanted her to be independent. To live her own life. To learn how to be an adult."

"So who do you think killed him?"

"I am completely stumped," said Paul. "I know, it looks like me. The rich guy protecting his daughter from a chiseler, but I didn't. I wouldn't have killed a man just to save my daughter pain. I simply would have cancelled our part in the wedding. Said no. If she wanted to do it, she had to do it on her own. I'd have taken the chance she would rethink things."

"But what if she didn't? What if she responded by eloping?"

"As I said, I was taking the coward's way out. Letting her learn her lesson the hard way. Which involved Maggie and I going along with things and waiting for Emma and Tristan to crash and burn."

"So, if you didn't do it, I can't see Maggie killing him either."

"No, Maggie, even when she's angry, doesn't lash out at others. And when she's not angry, she wouldn't hurt others. She catches wasps and hornets in a glass and takes them outside. Just to save their lives."

They continued walking out the other side of the garden, through an identical arch as the one they entered through. There was a short path through a maze of evergreen and deciduous trees before it opened out onto a view of a smooth wall made of gray stone. Or perhaps it was concrete. There were no seams like there would be for bricks. The opening into the garden was a moon gate. A circular entrance that gave a teasing glimpse of the garden within.

The Chinese garden was completely surrounded by the thick, sturdy wall. Or at least it looked like it was, as far as Gina could see. Three small brown buildings stood in different sections of the garden, blocking her view of where the wall would be. Each building had an elaborate roof that looked Chinese to her.

The two of them, followed the winding gravel path into the garden, passing beneath a blooming cherry tree. The pink blossoms had a sweet fragrance and the copper colored bark felt slick to the touch.

As they moved farther into the garden Gina heard water running and as she caught her first glimpse of a pond, a great blue heron lifted off and flew in the opposite direction.

"Oh," she said, startled.

"He comes every day, usually at dusk. He must be hungry earlier today," said Paul. The walked closer to the natural looking pond. A flood of mostly orange goldfish swam towards them.

"What a lot of fish," said Gina.

"Yes, they just keep breeding. The heron and kingfishers don't get all of them. They have hiding places."

Paul opened the lid of a brown wooden box and pulled out a plastic container of fish food. He tossed a couple of handfuls into the pond and there was a feeding frenzy.

Some of the goldfish were orange and white, others still had the black color of juveniles. Still others were white with orange, pale blue, and black spots. The largest ones were about six inches long. There were fat ones, skinny ones and others with long, elaborate tails and fins.

"We've only been feeding them for a couple of weeks. They've just woken up from winter," said Paul.

In one section of the pond sat a clump of yellow iris. They were the native iris, whose name escaped Gina at the moment. She just knew they were vigorous to the point of being a pest.

Out towards the center on the pond grew three different clumps of water lilies, not yet blooming, but their leaves looked unlike each other. Some plain green, others streaked with pink, the third clump, a deep purple-green.

"How deep is this pond?" she asked, pointing to the lilies.

"It's four feet deep. Those lilies are on islands that are a couple feet deep."

"And it's filtered? The water's so clear."

"Yes, we have a lot of filter on all our ponds. Gotta keep all those fish healthy."

As they walked through the garden Gina noticed that it contained more stone than plants. Massive boulders were perched among other smaller rocks to form the center of beds. Some had clumps of moss growing on them. Others were stacked.

As the path circled around the garden they came to a spot where the boulders looked truly foreign to her. They came in all shapes and sizes, but were light gray and deeply pitted. Many had holes that went entirely through the stone, making them look like they were formed of softly rounded Swiss cheese. Each boulder had a personality and ... gravitas.

"I've never seen stones like these."

"These are the rocks Maggie wanted for her fiftieth

birthday. Not diamonds, but limestone. These cost more than diamonds. They're from a specific region in China. The holes in them are caused from erosion, they soaked for millennia in an acidic lake. Traditional gardens in China have stones like these. Maggie wanted them too. I couldn't refuse her. Although, you wouldn't believe the paperwork and the money that had to exchange hands. Not to mention the shipping costs."

"They're amazing. I feel like each one should be the centerpiece of a garden."

"That's true, but I think they kind of like to hang out with other rocks," said Paul, smiling.

The garden had a few small rhodies and azaleas in full bloom, each one highlighted and surrounded by more local looking boulders, mostly gray, craggy and with no holes.

"How is Emma doing?" asked Gina.

"I think she's going to be all right. She's taking this very hard. Keeping to herself mostly. She's angry. I think part of her suspects that I'm responsible for Tristan's death, but she hasn't come out and said so. I'll be relieved when the murderer is caught. This whole thing has been so hard on all of us. I wish I could figure out who killed him. I can't see one of his business associates sneaking onto the island and being able to sneak poison into the port. Too many long shots."

"It didn't sound plausible to me either."

"But I can't figure out who on the island would have wanted him dead."

"Any ideas?" Gina asked.

"Well, Dustin has always had a crush on her, but she's half his age. And I've always have made it clear to all employees

that my daughter is completely off limits. As is my wife. And I just can't picture Dustin as a murderer."

Now that was interesting. She hadn't known Dustin had a thing for Emma.

"What about Martin?" asked Gina.

"Martin. I'd trust Martin with my life. Can't see him murdering anyone. Except for one time—our cook at the time was pissed off at him. She poured the contents of a pot of fish stock onto his bed. It smelled awful. He nearly did kill her, but I convinced him to fire her instead," said Paul, smiling.

"So Martin has firing power?" asked Gina. "Is that usual?"

"He manages the household staff, the cooks, housekeepers. I have final say in what he does, although I usually do things quietly and through him. Just to keep the pecking order clear to all the staff. I don't know if it's usual, but it seems to work here. He's always paying more attention to what goes or around here than I am. Especially if I'm traveling."

"What about Maggie?"

"She doesn't want any power. If she has requests, such a food she's craving, she usually tells the cook. Or if there a guests coming, she'll tell Martin. But she doesn't want to ha to manage anything in the house. Other than our soc calendar, which she's wonderful at doing. Keeps us all bi and entertained."

"So Martin couldn't kill anyone? Not even anyone who cheating on Emma, not to protect her."

"I can't see that. Wait ... Tristan was *already* cheating Emma?"

"That's what Emma told me."

"Who was it?" Paul's brows were wrinkled in anger.

"She didn't say. Just that Tristan told her the day th

died. She's feeling guilty because she should be mourning him and she's still angry."

"As she should be." Paul clenched his fists.

"Please don't let on that I told you. She told me in confidence."

"I won't. I have my own sources. Although, I'll need to get them to dig deeper. I want to know who it was."

"I'm sure the sheriff does too."

"Do you think he knows?"

"No, but the woman might be a suspect."

"Although again, we have the problem of someone sneaking onto the island and poisoning him."

"You're right. Not likely. So back to where we were," said Gina.

"Yes. Although I think I'll seek Emma out this afternoon. Spend some time with her. See if I can get the cooks to whip up some chocolate pudding and take it to her."

"Chocolate pudding?" asked Gina.

"When she was a little girl, it was her favorite comfort food. Guess she could use some comfort right now. I've been so busy trying to cancel all the wedding preparations and guests, I've nearly forgotten my daughter."

"I'm sure she'd appreciate it."

There was a gale of laughter that came from the driveway.

"Ah, they're here," said Paul. "Maggie's side of the family. Well, those other than Jennifer and Marsha. I'd know her mom's laugh anywhere. Buckle up and get ready for a ride," he said.

Gina smiled. A soft breeze brought the scent of the salt water from down below up to where they stood. The gardens

here were so massive it was easy to forget they were on a tiny island.

They left the Chinese garden. Gina decided to come back later and investigate all the little buildings. It was a charming place with all those beautiful boulders even though it wasn't her idea of a garden.

In the driveway, Martin was unloading large amounts of luggage onto a trolley. The front door of the house was open, so Gina assumed the guests had gone inside.

"Thanks Martin," said Paul. "Who's here?"

"This load was Maggie's Mom, Grandmother and Elizabeth. Your family is still down at the dock. "I'm going to pick them up as soon as I've got these unloaded."

"I'll take this inside and leave everything in the guest hallway. You can go back down to the dock and put things inside the appropriate rooms when you get back," said Paul.

"Thank you," said Martin, closing the trunk and getting back in the driver's seat.

Paul pushed the loaded trolley ahead of them and left it in front of the rooms that Gina supposed were empty. Then they turned around and headed to the parlor.

"Come on. You'd better get started meeting people before they all get here," said Paul. "I think it's time for a mid-afternoon pick me up."

There was much laughter coming from the parlor.

"Maggie's Mom's idea of dealing with death is to cheer everyone up and be the life of the party. She did that at her husband's wake. I was appalled at the whole idea until I got to know her. She's a kind soul who just wants to make everyone happy."

Gina followed him into the parlor, which still seemed

spacious even with all the people. Maggie sat on a couch between two older women. One who looked to be about ninety, with sparse short white hair, wore a navy pants suit.

The other woman, probably seventy with dyed red curly hair. Her eyebrows were also red, but three shades lighter, probably her natural color. The hair covering her head was more the color of cinnamon. She was plump like Maggie and wore black pants, a black, green and purple paisley blouse and lots of gold jewelry. Gina could smell her floral perfume across the room.

"Hello Gina," said Maggie. "This is my grandmother, Mary, and my mom, Margaret, and this is my Aunt Elizabeth," she gestured to a slender woman probably in her sixties with short maroon hair, who sat in a nearby chair. "She's my Mom's sister."

Elizabeth was dressed in black pants and a blouse with thin black and white stripes that melded into gray until one looked closely. She wore no jewelry and seemed glued to her cell phone.

"This is Gina Wetherby. She's an artist. She did that painting hanging over there, plus several in the dining room. We just love her work. She came over before the wedding, to bring the painting and to paint in our garden. And now we're trying to talk her into staying and painting. And staying and painting."

"Pleased to meet you," said Margaret.

"Hello," said Gina, shaking hands with each of them, Maggie's Grandmother last of all. The woman grasped Gina's hand with both of hers and held it for a time, patting it. In the way that Gina had noticed some older caring women do.

"Oh, it's so lovely to meet an artist," said Mary, with a slight accent which sounded vaguely familiar. "I love the colors you've used in that one. It's so pretty."

Tiffany walked around the room, taking drink orders and giving them to Julie, who was behind the bar making drinks.

Gina said, "I'd like something without alcohol."

Tiffany asked, "Iced tea?"

"Perfect."

"Sweet or plain."

"Plain, thank you."

Tiffany left for the kitchen, returning a few minutes later with a tall glass filled with ice, tea and a lemon slice perched on the edge.

Gina sipped it. The tea was black and fruity. The lemon added the perfect note to the flavor.

By then Paul's family had arrived. He introduced his father, Jonathon, a tall elegant man in a dark suit who looked about seventy.

His mother had shoulder-length brown hair and looked about sixty-five. She wore a suit with a skirt, a white blouse and low-heeled pumps. Around her neck was a short, tasteful silver pendant with a solitary pearl. She looked the epitome of class.

The third member of the party was a young man who looked like he was in his mid-thirties. He wore crisp jeans and black a t-shirt that read *It's not a bug, it's a feature*. And new expensive-looking running shoes. His head was shaved bald and he had a deep tan. Paul introduced him as Eric, his younger brother.

"Eric lives in Silicon Valley and creates software. He's the hippest of the hip."

"No, I'm way too old to be hip. If I was twenty-two, I might be hip."

"Long past your sell date then?" asked Paul.

"But still tasty," said Eric, grinning.

After drinks were all served, Gina noticed that Emma wasn't in the room.

"Has anyone seen Emma?" she asked.

Maggie said, "She wasn't feeling up to being around people right now."

"Poor thing," said Mary. "We're probably a bit too much for her."

"I'll go cheer her up later," said Margaret, laughter in her voice.

"I think she just wants to be alone," said Maggie. "Why don't you wait till tomorrow, Mom?"

"Killjoy," Margaret said.

Jennifer said, clearly attempting a diversion, "Mom, you'll have to come out to where Marsha and I had lunch today. The view's spectacular. And the weather is so gorgeous, for once."

"She's right," said Paul. "I don't remember a spring as glorious as this one. We've had so much sun, the garden's exploding with blooms."

"Oh, I'd love to go for a walk in the garden," said Mary. "A short one though. It's been a long day already."

"After we finish our drinks I'll show you around," said Maggie., "the roses aren't out yet, I know you love them, but the peonies are beautiful."

"Oh, I love peonies, too," said Mary.

Then the conversation in the room seemed to divide into two factions. Gina was in between the two families and tried to listen to both, but settled on the one between Paul's family.

"Have they found out who murdered the bridegroom?" asked Eric.

"No, the sheriff's still working on it," said Paul.

"It's been days and they still haven't arrested anyone?" asked Paul's father.

"No. They also haven't let anyone leave the island."

"Tristan's parents left. Martin told us," said Lillian.

"They didn't arrive here until after he was killed," said Paul. "They're not suspects."

"But you are? That's outrageous," said Jonathon.

"Dad," said Eric, "Everyone is probably a suspect until they catch the killer. The sheriff's probably just being careful. If he accuses the wrong person and let's everyone else go, then the real killer could vanish."

Paul said, "Exactly."

"Well, it's still wrong. To hold a man hostage in his own home," said Jonathon.

"I have nowhere else I'd rather be," said Paul "And I had no other plans. Emma was to be getting married, remember?"

Lillian put her hand on his shoulder, "I'm so sorry dear. Such a horrible thing."

"Yes, it is. Emma's heartbroken," said Paul.

Martin eventually joined them and took over the bar. He looked out of breath from moving everyone's luggage. After another round of drinks, dinner was announced.

FRIDAY EVENING

In the dining room, another table had been added to make it large enough. A longer lavender tablecloth had been put on them and the fancier china was laid out. Old fashioned bone china with a lavender floral pattern. The goblets had a silver flowery design around the top rim. Things had been fancied up for the families' arrivals. Three silver bowls filled with water and floating pink peonies were set along the centerline of the table.

Gina sat between Paul's Father, Jonathon, and Margaret's sister, Elizabeth.

Elizabeth owned an art gallery in Seattle it turned out. The one where Maggie had worked when she met Paul.

"I love your work," Elizabeth said. "I should do a show with botanic artists. I know it's not polite to talk business during dinner, but if I did such a show, would you be interested in participating? Should I send you an invitation?"

"Oh yes," said Gina. "I'd love to. But you'd need to give me a long heads up, so I had enough work ready to show. I tend to sell things as I paint and frame them."

"Well, how about next spring?" asked Elizabeth. "The gallery's booked solid all fall and winter. And one thinks of flowers and plants in the spring, even here in the Pacific Northwest where people garden year round."

"It's true. Next spring would be perfect. I'll set a few pieces aside. How many would you want from me?"

"Let's say ten. Nice round number. That way I can invite four other artists."

"Ten is doable. I better get busy though. I've promised several people paintings."

Gina sipped her iced tea, tasting the lemon which had grown stronger now after sitting in the tea for quite some time.

"I know Maggie wants to drag people around the garden tomorrow, but the weather forecast calls for rain."

"I can always find something to paint," said Gina. "I have a bouquet in my room. And large glass doors. Oh, and there's the glasshouse."

"And tomorrow was supposed to be the wedding. Such a shame, but now I guess it doesn't matter if it's pouring down buckets. Poor Tristan. Poor Emma."

"I know," said Gina.

"Are they even closing to finding out who the murderer is?" asked Elizabeth.

"Not that I know of."

"Well, it's not like this is a detective show where everything has to come out in the end. Real life is so often unsatisfying."

"True," said Gina.

The food arrived. It was surprisingly simple, given the place settings. Potato salad with a zesty mustard flavor, fried chicken which was moist on the inside, crispy on the outside, and a fruit salad of strawberries, watermelon, bananas and chopped fresh mint, all in a yogurt sauce. Everything tasted delicious.

Dessert was a chocolate layer cake, and a lemon layer cake. Gina chose chocolate. The cake was freshly baked, soft and dense with a rich, chocolate buttercream frosting. Maggie's family went mostly for the chocolate and Paul's for the lemon cake.

Dinner was over quickly.

Afterwards, the others went out to walk in the gardens in two different groups. Gina chose to retreat to her room. She was tired of making small talk with people. It had been a very long day. She was used to spending most of her time in solitude, except for the cats. Who didn't require talking to.

The only person she wanted to chat with was Sheriff Jansson. And for him to tell her that he'd solved the case. She was ready to go home.

That didn't happen.

So she watched a British detective show on the tv and went to bed early.

SATURDAY MORNING

Gina woke early to the sound of the pouring rain. It pounded on her windows. She opened the sitting room curtains and gazed out. Water streamed down outside and the wind was whipping past. She hoped the garden would be refreshed by the downpour and not battered.

She showered and dressed in jeans and a royal blue t-shirt. Slipped her sneakers on and went to the dining room.

A pale yellow tablecloth stretched over the tables, making the room appear brighter. The only person in the room was Jennifer.

"You're up early," she said.

"I went to bed early. The rain woke me up, I think," said Gina.

"Me too. Guess we'll be hanging out inside today. I've got some work to do. Today's a good day to do it, since I don't know if I'll get back to the office on Monday. I don't know when the sheriff will let us go."

"Neither do I. Have you seen him?"

"I saw him yesterday. He was out by the cabins."

"Cabins?" asked Gina. She tore open the small paper envelope containing a bag of English Breakfast tea.

"You know, where the staff live."

"Oh, I've never gone off that direction. I still haven't seen all of the garden," said Gina, pouring hot water over the teabag in her cup.

"It took me years of coming here to do that. And they kept adding more gardens on, so that didn't help."

Gina set the cup on the table, went back to the sideboard and dished up a cinnamon roll, two breakfast sausages and a spoonful of scrambled eggs with vegetables.

"I probably shouldn't eat so much," Gina said. "But everything's so good."

She sat in a chair across from Jennifer.

"It is, isn't it. I'm on my third cinnamon roll. And trying to figure out how I can kidnap Katie and take her to my house. To keep her happy and cooking, on my pittance of a salary."

"Katie makes the cinnamon rolls?"

"Yes she does. An old family recipe she says. I've never tasted a chocolate cinnamon roll before in my checkered past and I'm hopelessly addicted," said Jennifer.

Gina laughed. "I can understand that. They're amazing."

She took a bite of the hot sausage and the flavor erupted in her mouth. Meat, fat and salt. She closed her eyes, savoring the taste.

Martin came into the room, smiled and said, "Good morning." Then moved on to the kitchen.

"Morning," said Jennifer. "He's one busy man."

"How do you mean?"

"I heard him up last night at one in the morning, bringing

Paul's mother some ice for her aching shoulder. And here he is at seven in the morning. At work already. I don't think he sleeps."

"You were up at one?"

"I don't sleep very well at night. So, I nap a lot. It adds up to eight hours, just not all at once."

"Is Marsha still asleep?"

"Yes, she can sleep through nearly anything. Which is a good thing, cause I toss and turn a lot."

Gina nodded. She hadn't slept well last night. She kept wondering why there were no heavy lumps of cat on her bed.

About the time she finished eating, Maggie, Margaret and Elizabeth came into the dining room.

"Good morning," said Maggie. She looked terrible. Dark circles around her puffy eyes. The cheerfulness looked all put on.

"Are you okay?" asked Jennifer, her piercing eyes boring into Maggie.

"No. Not really. I thought this would be such a glorious day. The day my daughter was getting married."

Gina nodded. It must be such a disappointment.

"Have you talked to Emma lately?" asked Jennifer.

"I talked to her in the middle of the night. I came out to the kitchen for a snack. I found Emma here, making a cup of hot milk. Poor thing. She's grieving," said Maggie.

"Well, that's normal," said Margaret.

"Yes, it is. I talked her into doing something with all of us today," said Maggie.

"Mom will lift her spirits," said Jennifer. "Or Grandma."

"So, let's talk over breakfast and come up with something fun to do. I need coffee," said Maggie.

Gina excused herself, saying she had phone calls to make.

She didn't tell anyone about going to paint in the glasshouse. She needed more time alone before being sociable. And that feeling of guilt she got when being inactive for a long time nagged at the back of her brain. She needed to paint.

So, Gina gathered up her supplies and slipped her sweater on. Then snuck down to the front door and out. She ran down a gravel path, past the *Camellias* and into the side door of the glass house.

She was drenched from that short time in the rain, but the glasshouse felt warm and humid. She set her bag of supplies down on a wooden bench and took off her sweater, shaking it. Then brushing the water out of her hair as best she could. Gina slipped the sweater back on and wiped the rain off her face with a sleeve.

Over on one side of the glasshouse a frog began croaking. Another answered over on the other side. They began a back and forth chorus, both trying to attract a girlfriend. Female frogs didn't call, just the males. Gina didn't want to disturb them, so she didn't seek them out.

The glass house was lighter inside than the house had been. There were some grow lights on. Even in a glasshouse it was too dark during the Pacific Northwest winters, at least for tropicals. There were still heaters on in here. She stood in front of one of them, attempting to dry out somewhat.

Gina looked around trying to decide what to paint first. The pond with the koi was tempting, but whenever she moved close there was a flurry of nonstop motion from the hungry fish. She'd never capture that.

Finally, she settled on the spectacular wall of passion

flowers. Their sweet scent was a bit muted because the glasshouse had cooled slightly over the night. It would warm up during the day.

Gina set up her easel and watercolor block so the pad was horizontal for now. Then pulled out her paint. She poured water from her water bottle for painting, into a plastic cup and dipped a large brush into it. Smooshing the brush through some Payne's Gray paint, she added a bit more water, then washed the brush across the block. Gina repeated this until the entire paper was the pale, pale gray shade she was looking for. Then took a smaller brush and worked shadows into specific areas.

She rinsed the brushes and let the wash dry for a while.

Then went back in with a smaller brush and layered in several shades of green for the leaves. And black for the metal structure of the glasshouse.

Gina was just beginning to paint the stiff flower petals when she heard the rustling of raincoat and a deep voice.

"Oh, so this is where you're hiding," said Sheriff Jansson.

"Not hiding. Just working." Her voice was probably more brusque than she felt.

"Well, at least you're inside. It's raining frogs out there."

"As it should be," she said. "It's only April. They're in here too."

"Frogs? I don't doubt it. I got tricked by all that nice weather," he said. "So, you're really not hiding?"

She turned to look at him. His hair was all messed up from the hat he was holding, letting it drip on the gravel floor.

"Why? Should I be hiding?"

"Maggie said you were."

"Maybe I am. I didn't really want a roomful of people

following me out here to watch me work. Plus, I've run out of small talk. Being around that many people is exhausting."

"So, you're an introvert then?"

"Oh yes. I like people, but I appreciate my solitude."

"Well, you're out of luck, cause I have questions."

"Okay," said Gina, rinsing out her brush. She was down to the detail work and it didn't matter if the paper dried out. She wiped the water from her brush, set it down and walked over to one of the benches and sat down on the hard cast iron.

"Did you find out anything from Paul?" asked the sheriff, joining her on the bench.

"He said if he'd wanted to cancel the wedding, he and Maggie would have simply pulled out. Not paid for it, not hosted it. Left Emma and Tristan high and dry. Instead, they decided to move forward with it and let Emma learn a hard lesson about her choice in men. They figured it might take some time, but she'd be a wiser person in the end. He was also surprised that Tristan was already cheating on Emma. His sources hadn't told him that."

"Interesting."

"Does that mean he's not a suspect?"

"He's never been a very viable one," said the sheriff.

"What about Martin?"

"Martin is a mystery to me. I can't find anything out about him before he came here. It's as if he didn't exist."

"Paul said he'd trust Martin with his life. He must have some background on him or he wouldn't have hired him? I know, how about those witness protection programs. You know where someone goes underground?"

"No. They invent a history for those folks. This is different."

"Does he have a motive for killing Tristan?"

"Not that I can find. His story is like one of those old butlers you see on tv. Lives to serve the family, that sort of thing. Martin says he's very old fashioned."

Gina rubbed the hairy leaf of a potted *Tibouchina* which sat behind the bench. Beautiful purple flowers covered the plant, making it glow in the dim light from the darkly clouded sky.

"What sort of man would isolate himself from the world, live on an island with only a few people and live for someone else's family?" she asked.

"An emotionally damaged one, I'd think," said the sheriff.

"Enough to murder someone. Someone who was a threat to the family?"

"Possibly," he said. "I have no evidence."

"But if it was Martin, wouldn't he have found the body first and taken away all the wine. Destroyed the evidence?"

"Not if he was clever. By leaving it there, anyone could be implicated. Someone cleaning up afterwards would point towards him as the most likely suspect."

"Sounds like someone needs to have a talk with Emma. See who she thinks might have wanted to protect her, or just kill Tristan," said Gina.

"I've barely seen her," said the sheriff. "I'll need to go hunt her down, too."

"I think she's keeping to her rooms. Too many relatives. Who else are you trying to hunt down?"

"Gayle. She's either working or hiding. The last day it's been hiding. I haven't found her."

"Poor thing," said Gina. "She was really shaken up at seeing a dead body. Maybe I should go talk to her."

Just then, a gale of laughter echoed erupted just inside the door to the glasshouse and Maggie, Margaret, Mary and Jennifer came inside.

"Oh my, it is raining out there," said Margaret, her laugh filling the entire space.

"Well, hi Gina, Sheriff," said Maggie. "We didn't know you were in here."

"I came in to get out of the rain," he said. "Found Gina in here, painting."

"Oh, over here. This is just beautiful," said Margaret. She stood over by Gina's easel.

"It's not done yet. I still have a lot of detail work to do. Thought I better get going on some more paintings."

"Yes, you'd better," said Maggie. "Paul's just aching to spend money and buy more of your work."

"Well, I guess I should paint faster then," said Gina, laughing.

"It was nice chatting with you," said the sheriff. "I'll go back out into the deluge." He put his hat back on and zipped up his black raincoat. He tipped his hat at everyone and disappeared out the door and into the downpour.

Gina went back to her easel and looked at the painting. Only a few more brushstrokes and she finished it. Then carefully tore it off the watercolor block and lay it on an empty bench to finish drying. Moved the easel a bit closer to the wall of passion flowers. It was time to do an in-depth study of one flower. She laid down the wash for the background and let it begin to dry. Then loaded a smaller brush with a darker pinky-purple color, and began forming the flower.

"Has anyone seen Emma this morning?" asked Gina.

"No. She didn't want to come to breakfast," said Margaret. "I'm going to have to invade her privacy soon." She pronounced privacy, speaking the i like in privet. Was that an east coast thing?

She couldn't remember where Maggie had said her family lived, but she thought they were on the east coast somewhere.

"What about Gayle?" she asked.

Maggie said, "She's still doing poorly. Paul's thinking about bringing in a therapist to stay for a few months. Someone who works with trauma and grief. It would do everyone some good to talk this out, if they're willing to."

"I should think so," said Margaret. "I've never gone to a therapist myself. Never felt the need, but I hear it can be very useful."

Gina laid down the color for the petals and the center of the flower which was a dark brown, almost black.

"So Sheila is taking care of us all by herself?" asked Gina.

"I'm afraid so," said Maggie. "Every time Gayle tries to come back to work, she ends up being completely useless and Sheila tells her to go back to her cabin. Says everything Gayle does has to be redone. The girl can't seem to remember anything."

Gina said, "Maybe it's useful for Gayle though. To come and try to work. Try to get things back to normal."

"That's what I told Sheila. She said that Gayle needs to just leave the island. Go somewhere else where she has no history. She's looking at applications for other maids."

"That's very sad," said Gina.

"Yes it is," said Maggie.

A rush of cold air brought Paul, his parents and younger brother into the glasshouse.

"Oh hello, are we having a glasshouse party?" Paul asked.

"I guess we are," said Maggie.

"Oh, Gina's painting, I see the attraction now," he said.

Gina got a small brush and began to do the detail work, as everything she'd done before had now dried.

"Oh, that's very good," said Jonathon.

"Yes," said Lillian. "It looks just like those paintings you see in old books. Where they wrote the name of the plant next to it."

"Yes Mom," said Paul. "Gina's a botanical artist."

"I do stray sometimes," Gina said, "but thank you."

She hurriedly finished the last of the details and then rinsed her brushes.

"Well, that didn't take long," said Margaret. "You could paint a lot of those in a day."

"Decades of practice," said Gina, smiling. "And my old eyes get too tired to paint too much in a day. If I was still in my thirties, possibly, but then I wouldn't have had all that practice to know exactly what lines were necessary and which were too much."

"Exactly," said Paul. "She's got that down perfectly. Never a misstep in her paintings."

There were plenty of missteps in her work, but Gina felt pleased he hadn't noticed.

Margaret said, "I'm ready for a cup of tea. Shall we go back to the house?"

"Oh yes," said Mary. "I'm tired of walking. My poor feet need a rest."

"C'mon then, Mom," said Margaret, taking the older woman's arm. "Let's get you back to the dining room. Or the parlor."

"Oh, let's have tea in the parlor," said Maggie. "Give them time to clear and set up the dining room for lunch."

"Tea sounds refreshing," said Lillian.

"The parlor it is," said Paul.

"You coming Gina?"

"I'm still stuffed from breakfast," she said. "I'll see you at lunch."

Once they were all gone Gina finished the passion flower painting. Then she did a quick study of the pond with all the orange, red, yellow, white and black koi flashing through the water. She quite liked the way it turned out.

After that, she was done for the day. It was very warm and humid in the greenhouse. Maybe in the mid-seventies. It felt too hot for her at this time of year. Maybe in the heat of the summer it would have been fine, but for April, it was too much.

Gina packed everything up and walked through the garden to her room. It had stopped raining and everything smelled of damp soil and fresh air off Puget Sound.

She'd figured out how to get to the outside patio entrance from Dustin's map of the garden. There was one tricky path which looked like a dead end if you weren't paying attention.

Inside, she lay the paintings out on a table and spread out her sweater to dry on a straight chair.

The sheriff was going to talk to Emma. So was everyone else. Gina decided to talk to Gayle. See if she could help somehow.

She went to the bedroom and pulled out her khaki-colored hoody from the drawer. Slipped it on and zipped it up, pulling the hood over her head. She put the phone in her pocket and glanced at the map spread out on her bed to find the employees' cabins.

SATURDAY AFTERNOON

G ina left through her patio door, not wanting to run into any of the other guests for a while. She walked through the wet gardens, glad for wide gravel paths which kept her shoes mostly dry. There was only a light drizzle.

She went down the path leading past the new bed Dustin had been working on. All the plants had been arranged and planted in an ingenious arrangement. The species rhodies in full bloom, accented by the pink and white bleeding hearts. A common enough plant, but they were always showstoppers when in full bloom. There were plenty of blue-leafed *Hosta*. They were completely leafed out, unlike hers at home. Which hadn't spent all winter and spring in a greenhouse. Their leaves reminded her of seersucker fabric, all puckery.

She walked through the bamboo forest, which drooped beneath the weight of all the rain that had fallen. One stalk bent over so that she had to move it aside to walk down the pathway. She shook it and the stalk straightened, relieved of

155

the weight of the cold water, most of which ended up on her head.

Gina wiped the water off her face. She continued on towards the Japanese Garden, then instead of following it towards the house, took a path to the left which took her through a tunnel made of golden chain trees and *Wisteria*. A perfect mixture of lavender and yellow. The yellow chains of flowers dripped through the wire framework, mixed with the lavender grape-like clusters of the *Wisteria*.

The tunnel opened up to a gravel area and the cottages. Each of the cottages seemed to be landscaped differently.

The first one had a sign on the door which read *Martin Brooks* and was surrounded by highly pruned Japanese Maples and low growing evergreens. Their spring colors ranged from lime green to yellow to peach to a deep shrimp color.

Gina walked to the next building which had a cottage garden in front of it. She could see poppy, love-in-a-mist, and *Cosmos* seedlings. There were no evergreens. A couple of roses almost ready to pop into bloom sat in the middle of each side of the gravel path to the door. The garden was just the roses and lots of annual seedlings. In a couple of months it would be beautiful, right now it looked bare.

She knocked on the door of the white cottage. A short, stout woman with frizzy light brown hair answered. She looked about fifty.

"Hi, I'm looking for Gayle's cottage."

"Gayle's is the purple one. I'm Sheila. Can I help you?" The woman sipped a cup of coffee.

Gina could smell the grilled cheese sandwich which sat on the table next to the open door. Her stomach rumbled in response to the scent, which made her realize she'd skipped lunch.

"I'm Gina. I just wanted to talk to her, see how she was doing after discovering the body. She seemed so shaken up."

"She still is. I'm sure she needs to talk to someone, but she won't talk to me. Just starts sobbing and runs off. Poor thing."

"That doesn't help you much, does it?"

"No. And with all these guests, I'm way behind."

"Well, I'll let you get back to your lunch. You're doing a wonderful job. If it would help, you really don't have to wash my bedding and towels every day. It sure doesn't happen at my house."

"I don't know if I can lower my standards, but thank you for telling me. I'll consider it on the days I'm running short on time."

Gina turned and walked back down the the gravel path.

The purple cottage sat next to the white one. There was nothing growing in the exposed soil that lay in front of the building. A few rocks sat arranged in a two foot circle, as if someone had haphazardly tried to create something, but had little ambition.

Were the cottage tenants supposed to plant their own gardens?

Gina knocked lightly on the door and it opened on its own accord.

"Gayle?"

There was no answer.

She called again, "Gayle? Is anybody here?"

Nothing.

Gina turned the knob and surprised that it wasn't locked,

walked inside. She pulled the door closed behind her, so as not to let the warmth out.

The kitchen had an exposed wood beam crossing it, which was completely covered with drying herbs and flowers, hanging in upside down bundles.

The inside looked very earthy. Walls and furniture in greens and brown wood in contrast to the purple exterior. She checked the bathroom. Empty. And the bedroom, also empty of people. Gayle clearly still lived here. The bedding was all tangled and clothes lay strewn about.

She returned to the kitchen. A counter held opened mail, addressed to Gayle. All bills. Cell phone. Student loans. Gina examined the herbs. Most of them were dried flowers. Dusty, as if they'd been there all winter. Newer bundles of monkshood hung at one side of the beam. And a few other herbs that Gina didn't immediately recognize. Brand new foxglove stems with mostly opened blooms and the large lower leaves lay on the counter, wilting, next to a roll of string and some scissors. Waiting to be dried?

Digitalis purpurea, the area's native foxglove, was poisonous in the wrong amounts, heart medicine in the right amounts. Were these other flowers and herbs poisonous?

Had Gayle killed Tristan? Was she covering up her guilt by pretending to be shocked by his murder? Clearly, the sheriff needed to know about this.

Where was Gayle anyway?

Gina took another glance around, but found nothing that seemed out of place. She shouldn't linger. It wouldn't do to be discovered here.

She went out the front door, closing it behind her.

Then hurriedly crossed over the gravel area and to the *Laburnum-Wisteria* tunnel.

Just as she exited the tunnel, Gina ran into Gayle who was hurrying back to her cabin.

"Oh hello," said Gina. "I was just looking for you."

"Me, why?" asked the started girl.

"I haven't seen you around. I just wanted to see how you were doing."

"Fine, I'm fine," said Gayle, smiling a smile that didn't reach her eyes.

"Good. And listen, if you even need to talk to someone I'm available. I've been around a few years and sometimes people have said that I've collected a bit of wisdom. I'm a good listener."

"Thanks," said Gayle. She hurried past Gina, carrying a paper bag that looked like it contained groceries.

Did the staff cook their own meals? She should ask Paul.

In the meantime, Gina went in the hallway that contained the family's private rooms and took off her wet hoodie, shaking it to dry.

She knocked on the door that was Emma's, but there was no answer.

She thought for a moment about barging in, but Emma might be in there, just not answering. And what would she be looking for anyway? Other than the sheriff. Where were her manners?

Gina went back to her room and hung the hoody up to dry, swapping it for her now-dry cardigan, which felt stiff.

She texted the sheriff, saying, "*I have news. In my room, currently.*"

There was no immediate answer.

She slid her feet out of the wet shoes and set them by a heating duct, hoping they'd dry, but unsure if the heat would come on. She went into the bedroom and pulled out her pair of leather, or faux-leather walking shoes and a pair of warm socks. Ugly shoes, but functional. Her pants were fairly dry, so just changing socks and shoes should be enough to warm her. Then she looking in the mirror and tried to fix her mussed-up hair. It was damp enough to brush down flat.

She sat in the sitting area, noticing a bowl with a *Gardenia* floating in it on the table. The strong scent of the *Gardenia* didn't soothe her. Rather it revved her up even more.

She flipped through the pages of a book she'd brought with her, *Raven Black* by Anne Cleeves. A thriller or murder mystery depending on whose description you believed. At any rate, while it was a good book, it was definitely not what she needed right now.

In a short time, there was a knock at her door. She got up to answer it, finding Sheriff Jansson standing there.

"Oh thank goodness," she said.

"What's wrong?" he asked, coming in and closing the door.

"I went to Gayle's cottage." Gina described what she'd found.

"Now that's very, very interesting."

"Don't you think she must be the murderer?"

"I'd say there's a strong possibility. There could be other reasons she collected the herbs. We'll find out. I talked to Emma. She's doing fine, although she's spitting mad right now."

"Mad at who?"

"At herself, Tristan, the murderer. I'm sure she's not the murderer. Every second of her time is accounted for. Most of it was spent on the phone. Texting or talking to friends. Seems she was about ready to call off the wedding."

"So, we're down to Gayle and who else?" Gina asked.

He shrugged. A blast of sunlight shone through the windows, nearly blinding her.

"Well, I guess it's stopped raining out," said the sheriff.

"I guess so."

"I'm going to go talk with Martin," said the sheriff. He looked desperate and despondent.

"I think I'll go down to the Maggie and look at the walls of the main room. Paul said something about wanting me to do some paintings for there. I can't even remember the color of the wood."

After he left, Gina put on her dry sweater and headed off down the road to the docks. The air smelled fresh as if the rain had cleaned everything. Branches hung heavy with water. It would have been a terrible morning to be getting ready for a wedding. Still, having the bridegroom murdered was worse, despicable as he was. Poor Emma. Either way she was getting the raw end of the deal.

The road was well graveled and drainage so good, Gina didn't even get her shoes wet. Down at the docks she saw only the two yachts. The smaller power boat was gone. Where was it? No one was supposed to leave the island.

There was no police boat there, either. Had the sheriff left suddenly?

She went over the *Maggie* and yelled, "Hello."

"Hello," said Tom, emerging from below. "Can I help you?" He was wiping his hands on a rag and wore a dirty t-shirt and khaki pants, with a dark smear on them.

"Paul wanted me to paint some paintings to put in the main

cabin. I wanted to go in and look around. I can't remember what color the wood is or what sizes might be needed."

"Help yourself," he said.

Then she saw him look around and notice the missing boat.

"Was the *Lillian* here when you walked down the hill?"

"The *Lillian*, is that the power boat."

"Yes."

"No. Just the two larger boats."

"Damn, excuse my French." He took a cell phone out and called Paul.

Gina went inside the main cabin, but left the door open to overhear the conversation.

Not long afterwards she heard heavy footsteps running down the gravel.

"She can't have gotten far," said Paul. "Do you know how long she's been gone?"

"No. I've been down below all morning. Tuning up the engine." said Tom.

"Is she ready to go?" asked Paul.

"Yes."

"Let's take her, then," said Paul. "She's faster than the *Emma*. Not as fast as the little boat, but pretty close. I hope Gayle doesn't crash the *Lillian*."

"I shouldn't have let the deputy take the police cruiser."

Gina recognized the sheriff's voice. They rushed inside, past her. Towards the cockpit, barely acknowledging her presence.

"I don't feel good about bringing all of you along like this," said the sheriff.

"You're not bringing me along," said Paul. "I'm driving. No one pilots this boat, except me."

They took off slowly, but reached a fast speed quickly. Gina sat down on one of the chairs in the main cabin, watching the water rush past.

"Where would she go?" asked Paul.

"No idea. Probably Everett. There are places along the waterfront she can dock at. Does she have a car on the other side?"

"No, but I do. She might have taken the key. Here, take my cell and call Martin, ask him to check for the spare key."

"Do you where she's from? Where she might have friends or family?" asked the sheriff.

"Arlington, I think."

Gina could hear the sheriff talking on the phone, but couldn't make out the words. It was either a long phone call or he was making more than one.

"What's the make, year, color and license of the car?" he asked.

Paul said, "Fire engine red, Toyota 4 Runner. This year's model. Can't remember the license number. Martin can find it. I park it at a garage downtown. Martin can call them and have them detain anyone who tries to take the car."

There was more mumbling into the cell phone.

Gina could barely breathe. She was gripping the chair's arms and her heart pounded. Finally, she got up and went to the cockpit.

"Gina, what are you doing here?" asked Paul.

"I was in the boat when you came in. I came to look at the walls of the cabin. I was thinking about painting some seaweed and couldn't remember the wood color or how large they should be."

"I didn't even see you, sorry," said Paul. "You should sit down."

Gina sat at the dining table in the raised area behind the cockpit. Few boats moved across the Sound and they looked far away. She could see the mainland rising in the distance.

"How long till we get to Everett?" asked Gina.

"Forty-five minutes," said Paul.

"Thanks Deputy," said the sheriff, into his phone.

"News?" asked Gina.

"Gayle's former boyfriend, the one who she was heartbroken over, died from aconite poisoning. The Arlington police never did charge anyone. She was a minor, barely eighteen, and they didn't suspect her."

"There!" yelled Paul. "There she is!" He pointed to a tiny white speck far in front of them.

"How can you tell?" asked Gina.

Paul handed her a pair of binoculars.

Gina looked through them, but could only see a white boat with a covered area in front. She couldn't see who was driving it or a name on the boat.

"How can you tell it's yours?" she asked.

"I know my boats," Paul said, firmly.

"Can you catch her?" asked the sheriff.

"I don't know if I can before she docks," said Paul.

"If we can pinpoint where she's going to dock, I can have Everett police there waiting for her."

"I won't get too close then. Don't want to panic her."

Gina realized she was gripping the edge of the wooden table. She let out a deep breath and tried to relax.

"I'm not bringing you along on chases any more," said the sheriff.

"Why?"

"Looks like you're going to have a heart attack."

"Just letting off some steam so I won't," said Gina.

"This is a little tense isn't it?" asked Paul. "I can't believe she stole my boat. Ungrateful little wretch. And why would she kill Tristan?"

"We'll just have to ask her," said the sheriff.

It seemed to take forever to make it to Everett. Gina watched through the binoculars as Gayle stopped at one of the docks in the same area where the *Maggie* had been docked at. She left the boat carrying a large bag and ran up the steep gangplanks to the gate. She opened it and walked towards the main parking lot. Where four police officers grabbed her and handcuffed her.

Paul maneuvered the big yacht to the side of one dock and tied her off. Sheriff Janssen was off the boat and running before she even stopped moving. Gina followed him at a distance. He was a lot faster than she was.

When was the last time she'd run? Gina was out of breath by the time she reached the gate, Paul right behind her, not breathing nearly so hard. He was obviously in better shape.

Paul took her arm and they ran across the parking lot to where the police were talking to Gayle, and Sheriff Janssen stood.

"I hate you! I hate you all!" screamed Gayle. "No one cares about me. About my broken heart." Tears streamed down her red face.

The sheriff nodded and one of the police officers stuffed her into the back seat of a patrol car. He got in and drove off.

The sheriff spoke into his phone and then to the remaining three. Two of them left and the third one pointed to his car. The sheriff nodded and the officer went and sat in his car. It looked like he was typing things into a computer.

"What happens now?" asked Gina.

"We'll charge her with theft first. And for leaving the island when told not to, if we have to, in order to hold her. I'm 98% sure she's our murderer."

"What's the other 2%?" asked Paul.

"I can't find out anything about Martin's background. It's completely blank." The Sheriff stared at Paul.

"What is it you need to know?" asked Paul.

"Who he is."

Paul sighed deeply, then spoke quietly, "Martin grew up in a Christian cult. His parents were completely won over by their leader. They did anything he asked. Martin was abused, badly. Beaten and raped, as were all the children. He was a teenager when he escaped. I was coming home late one night, from a meeting and hit him with my car. He wasn't badly injured, a bit bruised. I took him to the emergency room, but the kid was terrified. Wouldn't give them his name. In the end I made one up for him so they'd at least see him. Afterwards, I asked him if he had anywhere to go. He didn't. So, I brought him home. Maggie took to him immediately. She loves to save lost souls. He took to her too. So we helped him enter the real world. Sent him to classes, then to the University. He's really smart. In the end, he wanted to stay with us. He's leery of people he doesn't know, although he hides it well."

"There's no record of any employment, no medical history, nothing," said the sheriff.

"We've kept everything very private. He's never worked for

anyone except us. Doesn't even have a social security number. He's not paying taxes, I know. He gives a lot of his income to charity. I figure it evens out. He's terrified that his parents or the cult leader will find him. Even after all these years. I'd appreciate if you could keep quiet about his past. He wouldn't be able to function in the real world," said Paul.

Gina stood in the parking lot, feeling the breeze blow past her. What kind of life was that, to be so afraid?

"So, he would never have killed Tristan? asked the sheriff.

"Well, he might have, but he'd have shot him or used rat poison. Something more common than, what was it? That strange plant?"

"Aconite. Aconite poisoning," said the sheriff.

"He wouldn't have used anything so obscure. That would narrow the field of possible murderers too much. Martin would be way too smart for that."

"Well, I'll see what Gayle has to say," said the sheriff. "I'm going to go down to the Everett station and interview her. I'll have someone drop me off back down here and I'll return your small boat to the island."

"Okay," said Paul. "Take care of her."

"You're going right back, correct?" asked the sheriff.

"If you say so."

"I say so. I haven't released anyone from leaving yet. Technically you two are in trouble."

"Then we'll return immediately," said Paul.

"I'll wait," said the sheriff, his arms folded across his chest.

"Oh, you mean now?" asked Paul, jokingly. He grabbed Gina's arms and said, "C'mon dear artist, I think we really should go now."

They walked back through the parking lot, down the

gangway and the dock. A seal swam between the rows of docks, looking hopefully at them.

"What's he or she looking for?" Gina asked.

"Sometime the fishermen throw their waste from cleaning their fish overboard. The seals love that."

"Of course."

They got back on the *Maggie* and Paul maneuvered her back out into open water. Gina sat beside him in the cockpit feeling rather numb.

Gayle. Who would have thought Gayle could have murdered Tristan? Or that Martin had such a sad story behind him? No wonder he seemed so standoffish and unapproachable.

The trip back to Frost Island seemed to take forever. Gina rolled things around in her head, trying to figure out why Gayle would have murdered Tristan. The only thing that made sense was if she was in love with Tristan. Had they had a fling? Had he returned her interest?

Gina didn't really want to talk. Paul didn't seem to have any conversation either. As they docked, he said, "I'm afraid I'm not being a very good host."

"Well, things have been a little strange," she said, "but not dull."

Before they got out, Gina snapped a few photos from inside the yacht. She'd need to research seaweed, having never paid much attention to it before.

Martin was waiting for them in the car. They climbed in and drove up the hill.

"Do the others know what's going on?" asked Paul.

"I'm afraid so. Maggie overheard you and the sheriff. News has spread like wildfire."

"Okay, gather everyone in the parlor, staff included, and I'll make an announcement in fifteen minutes."

"Will do," said Martin, a grim look on his face.

When the car stopped at the front door, Gina crawled out. She'd been sweaty from running and it had dried. Her clothes must stink.

She headed towards her room at the center of the building.

"You are coming, aren't you?" asked Paul.

"Yes. Just going to go change."

"Fifteen minutes."

She nodded and hurried to her room. She did a quick sponge bath with a washcloth and changed into clean capris and a t-shirt. Her other shoes were dry so she slipped them on with a clean pair of socks. Then smoothed her hair down again, tucked her phone in her capris' pocket and went out the door.

Ten minutes.

SATURDAY EVENING

The parlor was full of people. All of Maggie's family and Paul's. Even Emma was there, looking better than when Gina had last seen her. The staff stood clumped together, except for Martin. All of them present, even Tom, whom she'd never seen away from the boats. The only one missing was Paul.

Martin was behind the bar, serving wine, beer and sodas.

Gina went over to the bar and asked, "Do you have whiskey?"

"Of course. Straight?"

"A few drops of water if possible."

"For you, anything is possible," he said, smiling.

Gina looked into his eyes. It was a genuine smile. She returned it.

He handed her the tumbler which had more than one finger of whiskey in it. Gina sipped the liquid which was the precise color of a deep gold watercolor she'd ordered last week. The whiskey had a strong flavor, followed by a number of complex tastes she couldn't put a name to. It warmed her inside and she suddenly felt flushed.

"What do you think of all this?" asked Jennifer. "Poor Emma having to live through all this again. And on what would have been her wedding day."

Gina looked over at Emma, who sat on the couch, wearing a black t-shirt and jeans. She looked in complete control. Her great-grandmother sat on one side and her Aunt Elizabeth on the other. They hugged and patted her. Making much of her. Somehow, Emma was glowing, thriving on all the attention.

Paul stepped into the room and everyone quieted.

"I just want to thank you all for coming. This is not quite the day we'd expected to celebrate today, but we're comforted to be surrounded by family and friends. As many of you heard, it is looking like Gayle poisoned Tristan. We don't know why, perhaps we never will."

Gina's phone vibrated and she made her way out into the hallway, pulling it out with one hand. It was the sheriff.

"Hello."

"Hi Gina. I just thought you would want to know. Gayle has confessed to killing Tristan. And her late boyfriend, as well. Hopefully, she'll be locked away for a good long time."

"Why did she do it?"

"She and Tristan were having an affair. He told her he loved her, but wouldn't leave Emma. Gayle got mad and poisoned him so Emma couldn't have him."

"It's odd that she didn't poison Emma, isn't it?"

"Gayle's not the most well-balanced of people. She'll have a psych eval, of course. Well, I'd better go, I need to call Paul."

"Thanks for letting me know," she said, hanging up and putting the phone in her pocket. Gina stepped back into the parlor. She sipped more whiskey, which tasted really good. As her muscles relaxed a bit, it became clear to her how on-edge she'd been ever since the murder.

A few seconds later, Paul's phone rang. He stopped talking and answered the phone. He asked a few questions and hung up.

"Well, that was the sheriff. Gayle has confessed. He'll have a couple more things to do out here tomorrow. After that those of you who want to leave will be able to. Although, there's no hurry. We've got a lot of food out there in the cooler and the cooks have only just got started with inventing new things to do with it. You are all welcome to stay as long as you wish. I think Emma and Maggie could use the support. I know I could. And now, I'll dismiss the cooks, because dinner is about to be served. If I can have the rest of you move on to the dining room."

Dinner. What happened to lunch?

At the mention of food, Gina's belly growled. She hadn't eaten since breakfast and here she was drinking whiskey. She'd be drunk before finishing the glass.

Gina carried it with her into the dining room and sat down close to Jennifer and Marsha.

She didn't remember much about the dinner, except that there was an overwhelming feeling of relief and gaiety about it. Paul's mother and father seemed to be a bit stuffy about the whole thing, not comprehending how everyone else felt.

The meat, steak and lobster were grilled to perfection and sat alongside wild greens dressed with olive oil, balsamic vinegar, oregano and fennel. There were rosemary roasted potatoes and carrots on the side. Strawberries from a greenhouse were laid over chocolate ganache in a tart shell and topped with whipped cream.

Gina thought she would burst. She finished her whiskey, then had a glass of dessert wine. A fruity ice wine from Eastern Washington, that felt so thick as to be syrupy, but tasted crisp and fresh.

She decided not to linger with people in the parlor and returned to her room. Her head was swimming. She kicked her shoes off and sank down on the couch in her room. It had been a very interesting few days.

Tomorrow, she'd pack, take a few more photos and get on the boat home.

SUNDAY MORNING

The next morning, Gina joined the others for breakfast. Her last chance at the chocolate cinnamon rolls. The cooks had made those as well as cream cheese Danish and croissants filled with bittersweet chocolate. There were scrambled eggs with cheese and vegetables, sausages, bacon, potatoes and toast for those who preferred more savory offerings.

After breakfast, the sun was shining so Gina walked through the gardens, returning the map to Dustin's bulletin board. He was nowhere to be seen. She took photos of the places she wanted to paint. The garden looked brighter for yesterday's heavy rainfall. Everything clean and fresh. The sun's heat brought out the fragrances of the lilacs, peonies and the first sweet peas, which must surely have been started in a greenhouse and brought outside to bloom more than a month early.

It was a delightful walk, something to see around every curve. Then again, Dustin had most likely planned for the garden to peak in time for the wedding. There was obviously lots more to come throughout the spring and summer, but the everything looked glorious now.

She ran into the sheriff in the Japanese Garden. He was coming from Gayle's cottage, a grim look on his face, until he saw her.

"Well, hello," he said, his face lighting up.

"Hello. How are you?"

"I've been better. I'm relieved to get this solved at least. Just on my way to ask Paul and Emma a few more questions, and let everyone go. I assume you're going back."

"Yes. I'm looking forward to going home."

"I'm going back over on Paul's boat. I need to leave our boat here with the deputies. I have to be in Coupeville to testify tomorrow morning."

"That's a lot of traveling," said Gina.

"Part of the job description," he said. "Anyway, I can give you a ride home if you need one. I have a car parked over in Everett."

"I'd love a ride. Melanie will be relieved she doesn't have to cram me into her schedule today."

"Great. I think Paul's taking people over just after lunch."

"I'd better go get ready then."

Gina went back to her room and packed her clothes, charger and toiletries. Her bag seemed fuller now. Must be all the dirt. She hadn't added anything.

She took one last look around the beautiful room, sniffed the sweet *Gardenias* on the table, shouldered her purse and the painting bag. Then she pulled her suitcase down the hall. Martin was rolling a luggage rack into the center of the building.

"I'll take that ma'am," he said.

"Only if you don't call me ma'am. Makes me feel older than I already do."

He smiled and bowed.

"Our most gracious and talented artist then, how's that?"

"Far too grand. How about Gina?"

"Gina, it is," he said. "I hope you'll come back. Maggie gets so lonely. Next time we'll try to avoid having a murder."

"I'd like to come back. When the roses are in bloom."

"The roses are spectacular. And so are the *Hydrangea*. And then there's the fall color. Even in winter the garden is wonderful."

"I'll see what I can work into my schedule. I've got a lot of painting to do, obviously."

Lunch was simple. Grilled tuna or cheddar cheese sandwiches, green salads and iced tea or lemonade. For dessert it was homemade ice cream in lavender, chocolate or vanilla. Gina had all three.

The sheriff joined them for lunch. He sat next to Paul and his father. Gina couldn't hear what they were talking about.

Paul was taking Jennifer, Marsha, the Sheriff and Gina back after lunch. Maggie talked to Jennifer, Marsha and Gina.

"Oh, I do hope all of you come back soon."

"I know, rough deal leaving you with Gran, Mom and Liz," said Jennifer, "but I've gotta get back to work."

"Me too," said Marsha.

"But we'll come back, we always do."

"And you'll come back, right Gina? I'll need some help planning that garden tour. I've never even been on one."

"I'd love to come back. I really want to see the garden in another season."

"Oh, it's lovely. And you'll have paintings to deliver, right?"

"I expect I will. Not sure when though."

"Anytime is just fine."

Gina felt relieved to get on the boat. She rode in the main cabin, looking at the walls and trying to avoid the chatter of Jennifer and Marsha. She was really talked out and there was the hour long car ride with the Sheriff left to go.

Then it hit her. She'd seen photos of a wine colored seaweed that grew around here. That would be the perfect color for these walls. If she could find four different varieties that had diverse shapes it might work perfectly. Or even two different varieties in different seasons. Did seaweed change during the seasons? Two paintings for each side wall. By the time she had it all worked out, they'd reached Everett. She said goodbye to Paul, Jennifer and Marsha up in the parking lot and promised to come back again.

"Maggie really wants to be on a garden tour, but I'm afraid she needs a little hand-holding," said Paul. "She's nervous."

"I'll see what I can do," said Gina. "Gardeners are a great group of people. Most of them are just nice folks. She's going to do fine."

"I know that and you know that. She doesn't. Call me when you have paintings done. I'll be happy to pick you up any time," he said.

Gina followed Sheriff Jansson to the patrol car, which was a small SUV. He put her suitcase and painting bag in the back seat and she got in the front. In the center of the front was a platform with a computer attached to it.

"I remember when police cars didn't have computers," she said. "When no one had them."

"So do I," he said. "But they help us so much. It makes

paperwork so much easier. And I can find out if the driver of the car with the broken tail-light I'm stopping has any warrants. It gives me a little forewarning. Sometimes."

The drive went by faster than she expected. He talked about his brother's family. All the nieces and nephews and their kids who he had to play with.

"So you never married?"

"Never found the right woman. Or rather I found them, but they didn't want me. Being married to a cop doesn't bring with it long-term relationships. Not usually. The divorce rate is pretty high and the higher up you rise, the more complicated things get. As sheriff, I'm always on call. The deputies rotate on and off. Not me."

"That's hard. But aren't you nearing retirement?"

"Yeah, but what would I do? I've gotten smarter over the years. I've still got some years of usefulness in me. I'm not ready to let go of this job yet and my supervisors tell me I'm still doing a good job. So, I'll stay on for a while yet. You're not ready to hang up the paintbrush are you?"

"Not at all, but this is my second career. It feels like I just started it."

"True. What did you do before?"

"I was the marketing director for a small chain of gift shops in Seattle."

"I don't see you as a marketing director."

"What? I don't look the part in dirty wrinkled capris and t-shirt?"

"No. It just seems like a job for someone who's ... ordinary. You and your paintings aren't ordinary. You're an artist. One of a kind. You don't think inside the box."

"Good marketing directors think both inside and outside the box."

The car turned off I-5 and onto the road which led to Raven Island. Half an hour later they were at her house. He parked in the driveway and unloaded her suitcase.

"Hey, how would you like to meet for coffee some morning? If I ever get a day off," he asked.

"That would be lovely, but I need to know, what type of meet for coffee?"

"What kinds are there?" he asked, his face wrinkled as if he was puzzled.

"There's the *I need to talk to someone* kind. The *I need a friend* kind. Also, the *I want to sell you something* kind."

"No, none of those," he said. "This is more the *I really like you, I think we could be more than friends, but it's been so long since I had a date, I don't know what to do anymore and I have to take things really slow* kind."

"Oh, that kind. Good to know."

"Does it make a difference?" he asked.

"Yes, if you were trying to sell me something, I'd say no."

He laughed.

Gina got her keys out and unlocked the front door.

"Hello," she said, loudly. "Shelley."

"Mrooow, mrooooow," said Alice, winding around her ankles.

The sheriff had followed her in with her suitcase and paint bag. He closed the door, quickly so as not to let the cats out. The house smelled like home, but had a closed up smell. Shelley hadn't opened the windows.

The guest room door opened and Shelly came out, her long hair messed up.

"Mom, you're back." Shelley held out her arms and hugged her.

"It's so good to see you," said Gina.

The hug felt wonderful. Her daughter was strong.

"Oh, you've got company," said Shelley.

"This is Sheriff Janssen. He brought me home," said Gina. "This is my daughter Shelly.

"Sheriff," said Shelley, shaking his hand.

"Bryan, please," he said.

It was then that Gina realized she'd never asked his first name. Ever. What a dunderhead she was.

"Well, I'd better get going. I need to go over some papers at the station before I head home," he said.

"You really need to go in?" asked Gina.

"Unfortunately yes. I can't remember much about the case I'm testifying on tomorrow. I need to reread things and remember."

"Okay. Well, give me a call when you've got a day off and we'll see about that coffee."

His eyes lit up and he smiled. "I'll do that." He went back out the door.

Gina said to Shelley, "I'm going to make some tea, would you like some?"

She poured water into the teakettle.

"I'd love some. Then you can tell me about your big adventure."

"And you can tell me about yours."

"Mine's anticlimactic and overwhelming. I'll tell you tomorrow. With photos, because India's lovely and horrible all at the same time."

"Just like everywhere. Wait, I thought you were in Indonesia."

"I was there too," said Shelley. "I was everywhere."

Shelley pulled out teacups and Gina filled a teapot with strong black tea. Albert got off the couch and came over to say hello. Both cats waited by the empty food bowls. She fed them, an hour early and opened the kitchen window a crack to let in the spring breeze. Then kicked her shoes off.

Home again.

Things might not be exactly the same as usual, but they were good. Very, very good.

KATIE'S SUPER SECRET CHOCOLATE CINNAMON ROLLS**

Preheat oven to 375 °F, Makes 12 rolls

DOUGH:
3/4c. warm water
1 Tbls. or 1 pkg. dry yeast
1/4c. butter, melted
1 tsp. salt
1/4c. sugar
1 egg, beaten
1/4c. cocoa
2-1/4c. flour

FILLING:
1Tbls. butter, melted
2tsp. cinnamon
2tsp. sugar

GLAZE:

1/2c. powdered sugar

1Tbls. milk, or enough to make a medium thick glaze

Dissolve yeast in warm water, add melted, cooled butter, salt, sugar, egg, cocoa and 1c. flour. Beat well. Stir in remaining flour. Blend well.

Place in greased bowl and cover with cloth or plastic wrap and let rise in warm place (85°) for one hour.

Turn soft dough out on floured board. Roll 12"x19" square. Spread with melted butter. Sprinkle with cinnamon and sugar. Roll up, beginning at a wide side, trying to keep the entire roll the same width. Cut into 12 equal pieces. Put the pieces into a greased 8"x8" pan, with spiral side up and press gently so the rolls are the same height. Let rise 40 minutes or until double. Bake 20-25 min. until tops begin to brown and centers of rolls feel firmish. Drizzle glaze over the top.

Don't eat them all in one sitting!

**Okay, confession time. These aren't Katie's rolls, because she's a fictional character. They're mine. Once upon a time, when I was a young impressionable girl, my mom signed me up for 4-H. I was thinking Yay! Dogs and horses.

No, it was cooking and sewing. Sigh. However, I did get this recipe out of it, from my 4-H leader, whose name has long since escaped my mind. So, I'm calling them mine. And they are amazing. And yes, I have eaten them all in one sitting. On more than one occasion.

ABOUT THE AUTHOR

Linda Jordan writes fascinating characters, visionary worlds, and imaginative fiction. She creates both long and short fiction, serious and silly. She believes in the power of healing and transformation, and many of her stories follow those themes.

In a previous lifetime, Linda coordinated the Clarion West Writers' Workshop as well as the Reading Series. She spent four years as Chair of the Board of Directors during Clarion West's formative period. She's also worked as a travel agent, a baker, and a pond plant/fish sales person, you know, the sort of things one does as a writer.

Currently, she's the Programming Director for the Writers Cooperative of the Pacific Northwest.

Linda now lives in the rainy wilds of Washington state with her husband, daughter, four cats, a cluster of Koi and an infinite number of slugs and snails.

Her other work includes:
Horticultural Homicide
Murder at the Rosewood
A Hanging Offense
Continental Divide
Notes on the Moon People

Living in the Lower Chakras
All her work can be found at your favorite online bookseller.

Get a FREE ebook!
Sign up for Linda's Serendipitous Newsletter at her website:
www.LindaJordan.net

Visit her at: www.LindaJordan.net
She can be found on Facebook at:
www.facebook.com/LindaJordanWriter
Metamorphosis Press website is at: www.
MetamorphosisPress.com
Goodreads: https://www.goodreads.com/author/show/
2021274.Linda_Jordan

Writers love reviews, even short, simple ones and honest
reviews help other readers find the book. Please go to where
you bought this book, or Goodreads, and leave a review. It
would be much appreciated.